THE HALF-BLESSED

SPECIAL EDITION

A NOVEL

A.L. YOUNG

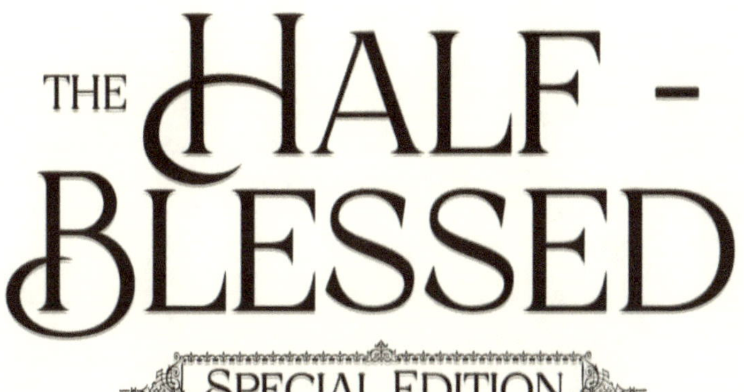

A NOVEL

A.L. YOUNG

The Half-Blessed

Book One

The Blue Lattice Network

A. L. Young

ISBN(Paperback): 979-8-9880030-1-4

Copyright © 2023 by A. L. Young

All rights reserved.

No part of this book may be reproduced in any form or by any electronic or mechanical means, including information storage and retrieval systems, without written permission from the author, except for the use of brief quotations in a book review.

This is a work of fiction. Names, characters, places and incidents either are the product of the author's imagination or are used fictitiously, and any resemblance to any actual persons, living or dead, events or locals is entirely coincidental.

Cover design by Get Covers

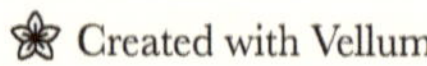
Created with Vellum

For all of us with stories that want to bring them to life

Letter from the Author

Dear Reader,

Due to the dark nature of the book, certain warnings should be made. This book contains graphic depictions and mentions of drug use, adoptee trauma, closed door sex, mild to serious police encounters, mass child death, the death of a parent, parental manipulation and coercion, chronic lying, bribery, chronic pain, gore and blood. If you are sensitive to such material, proceed with caution. Your mental health matters. This is not an exhaustive list but one to the best of my ability from reflection on the writing of this piece. I would also like to add that I appreciate your buying or borrowing or choosing my book from a little library and giving my story the chance for you to encounter another world. It means so much to me as an indie author to get the opportunity to tell my story. I hope I can meet your expectations. If you find aspects of the book that you feel should be added to the list of trigger warnings please email: alyoungwrites@gmail.com so I may compile them and add them to subsequent revisions. I will also add them to my website.

Thank you again, dear reader

-A.L. Young

Cadril

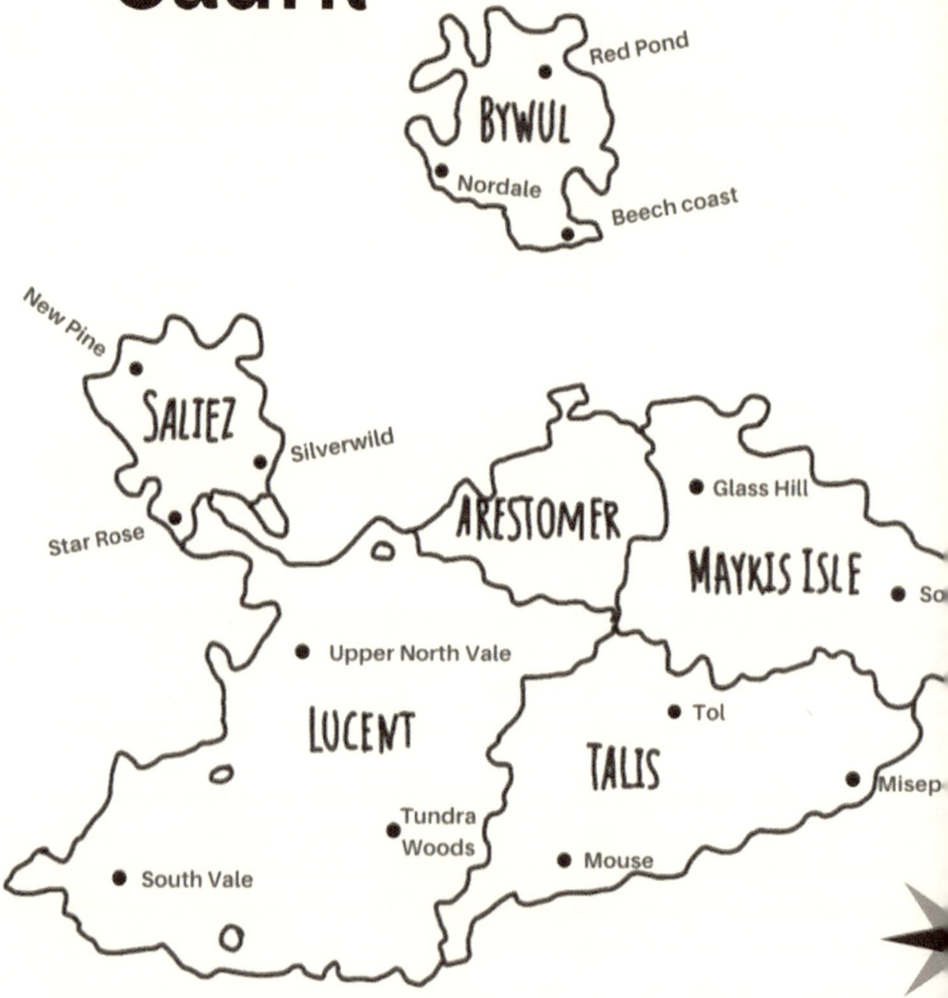

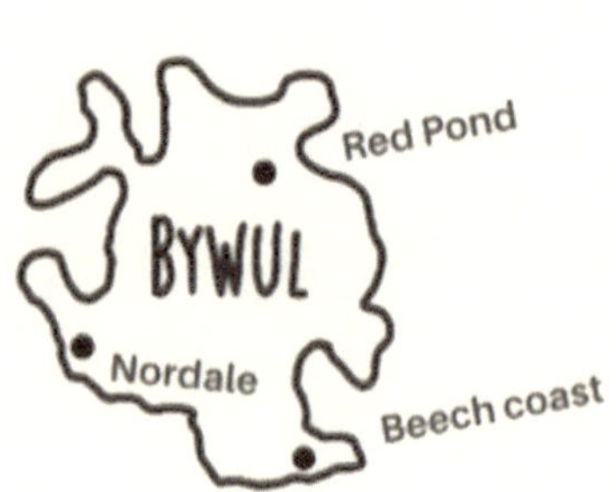

BYWUL
Red Pond
Nordale
Beech coast
New Pine
SALIEZ
Silverwild
Star Rose
ARESTOMER
Glass Hill
MAYKIS ISLE
Upper North Vale
LUCENT
Tol
TALIS
Misep
Tundra Woods
Mouse
South Vale

Crow Feather
Willow Port
Boye
RAVEN
CROW
May Hills
Cedar Wood
Diamond Sea
GRASSHOPPER
South Hills
Turpeek
Amaryllis
City Center
Moss Point
Ocul
ROBIN
Bayville
BLUEBIRD
EAGLE
Bell
Whispers
Clayton
Anvil
Lance Bank
Ivy Ladder
Kroft
PHOENIX
Hush

Contents

PROLOGUE

Amethyst: April 4, 2071

Amethyst found the monotony of scanning groceries a welcome change to memorizing formulas. Each soft beep was a disruption of any thought that was bothering her, including the long essay that was due in a week for sociology—*beep*—the leak that couldn't yet be fixed at the back of the store—*beep*—the heart condition her father had that was getting worse—*beep*. It was easy for a moment to put away these thoughts.

The line was an aisle long and included some of her impatient classmates, buying their lunches at the supermarket instead of the café. These poor souls had Saturday classes. She was saved from that fate because she wasn't too bad at English or math. She was nearly done with the line when she heard someone yell, "Help her!"

Outside, a large gathering of people was forming. They were talking to one another. They were asking questions too fast. They were taking out their cell phones. In the store, she heard a similar commotion next to the fridges. She couldn't see what was happening, but she did see a tall man wearing gym shorts say, "She just fell out of nowhere." And a group of people surrounded what looked like a student. The girl was wearing a uniform of saddled oxford shoes, green plaid skirt, and a white polo, so she wasn't from Amethyst's school but from one nearby.

Some of the people in line froze. Amethyst motioned them forward, and the woman in front let the man behind her go forward so she could walk over to the girl lying near the fridges. She said, "I'm a nurse." And she began trying to see if the girl would wake.

Amethyst kept scanning to keep the line moving. She didn't know what else to do. She was about to charge the man for his three items, but the two girls standing in line with their sandwiches fainted, falling hard onto the linoleum. Amethyst's hands trembled. Her heart raced. The man stood there, stunned, and then crouched down beside them, trying to get them to wake.

"I . . . I have to call my manager. I'm sorry," Amethyst mumbled as she walked over to the phone on the wall toward where the other girl fell.

"Rob, there's a couple of sick girls in the supermarket. What do I do?" She heard the tears in her voice, and through the receiver, she could hear him breathe deeply and exhale.

"I called emergency services. They're all tied up. It's happening all over town. They just told us to keep them comfortable."

"She's dead!" someone shouted.

"I'll be there in a minute," her manager said. "There's a guy here who seems to be half awake. Tell Rochelle to come to aisle 7."

"Rochelle to aisle 7. Rochelle to aisle 7."

Rochelle ran down to aisle 7 faster than Amethyst had ever seen her move. She worked at the back of the store, handling the shipments. There was a crowd now surrounding the girls who fell in front of her register. The man was waving his arms, she guessed in an attempt to keep people at a distance.

Amethyst walked back over and saw a clear view of what they looked like. She would never get the image out of her head. Their faces were blue, like they had suffocated, and the corners of their mouths had blood dripping from the sides as well as from their nostrils. The man shook his head. He put his hands to his mouth, cupping it. He began to cry.

"I'll call them again. I'll call them again." Amethyst called emergency services, and when she got through, they told her they would arrive after twenty minutes and that a lot of episodes were being reported around the territory. By the time they did arrive, the girl who had fallen outside had her face covered with a black leather jacket. She wore the same uniform Amethyst was wearing—a navy blazer, blue and yellow plaid skirt, and cream blouse.

The store emptied. EMTs arrived. Amethyst stood by the bread aisle, looking at the top of the girls' heads. The EMTs were looking them over side by side, and when they determined what had occurred, the three girls and one guy were put on stretchers and covered with white sheets.

One of the EMTs asked Amethyst to "please keep off the road" as she left. She walked to the back office, where she kept her things, grabbed it, and left. She didn't know what to expect. What she encountered was much of the same of what she saw inside—people around her age lying in the street, surrounded by adults. Some of them had already been covered by sheets, and every few blocks or so, there were officers keeping crowds from forming around the bodies.

She walked down the city center the fastest she ever did, nearly running and trying her best not to see anything. She focused on the bright red turret of her apartment complex that stood on the boundary of the city center and the suburb. She couldn't calm her nerves when she had to open the lobby door. The key card shook in her hand, and she kept dropping her keys for her apartment door. She thanked whatever controlled the universe for not showing her anything else horrible.

The news that night was scary. Arnett, her mom, saw a group of students collapse on the bus, and she immediately thought they fell from the turn and not because they were critically ill. They waited as the news channels seemed to catch up with what was happening. The news was just labeling it as asphyxia, but Amethyst could not understand why the girls she saw had nosebleeds. Every news channel said the same thing, that they didn't know what caused it and that maybe it was an illness spreading through the schools. Most of the people affected were her age, and the thought of it happening to her was terrifying. Then she had another thought. Why *hadn't* it happened to her?

Amethyst sat in front of the television, trying to absorb everything, watching each loop of the news story, holding on to the promise there would be more information. At 4:15 a.m., the event was given a name, "the Falling."

RUN: MARCH 15TH

Amethyst

News had been spotty for most of yesterday, the radio towers losing their reach after fifteen-some odd miles. They had officially entered a dead zone. The last bit of news yesterday afternoon was an announcement that the Lost Children had staged a protest in the lobby of Hunter's Point Mall in Ivy Ladder and what sounded like hundreds shouting, "Let us out! Let us out!" over a loudspeaker. This had happened on March 13, but news stations said nothing about it until the next day. This was just another tactic to keep students in line and not too "excited." Or rather inspired by what was happening, they couldn't rein all of them in.

The sound bite crackled and popped like it was an old newsreel. The sound of gates being drawn and guns discharging on the sound bite rattled inside Amethyst's head for miles. The station went silent before they could find out what side the shots came from.

The pair wove through the mountains that hugged Moss Point; the heavy smell of sap baking in the hot air filled the SUV. Moss Point was a larger town in the Bluebird Territory just north of Bluebird Stream, the town Amethyst was from. Amethyst's mom had gotten them this far, and at their current pace, they would reach Arestromer in three days. In that moment, she was measuring the time by how many breaths she could get past her lips without her mom realizing her stomach was in knots. This pain was nothing new and because of this whenever it hit her, she tried her best to keep quiet and not worry her mom. She had her methods for keeping it tame. She would breathe deeply, swallow about 1000 mg of extra strength pain killers and hope it would go away sooner rather than later. That was all she really could do.

She had this constant ache for close to two years now, and all a typical doctor could do was guess what it was as there was no physical indication that anything was wrong with her body. It was suggested by one of the last doctors she saw before they left that it was psychological. She can't remember his name because she was in so much pain at that appointment. Most of the time, the pain she had was manageable; but other times, it was like being hit in the head with a hammer and the impending dizziness and darkness that would follow. It was like her body couldn't contain the pain, and it just ripped her from the inside, trying desperately to create more space. That wasn't one of those times, but nonetheless, her mind was occupied with when it would end.

Her mom looked straight ahead, letting a man merge in from of them. "We're getting close to a burger place. Your turn to eat."

She looked up and nodded. "Hm," which in her language meant "Yes, burger sounds good, and I am OK with stopping." She couldn't help but to lie.

The members of the Authority were jumpy. Fleeing from the lockdown had become so commonplace that they were questioning everyone. Producing papers indicating Bluebird citizenship was an easy way to be taken in for questioning. There were over four thousand citizens who were due to have their citizenship expire because of a new law that deemed the foster children from the Crow Territory no longer citizens on January 1, 2074. They were temporarily relocated to the Bluebird Territory as children so they wouldn't starve because of the famine.

The famine was long since over, but older laws had complicated the situation. Anyone, regardless of whether they did paperwork or not, was a citizen if they lived in the territory for more than ten years. Instead of reaching an agreement with the Crow Territory president Luke Talis and the Bluebird Territory president Xavier Snow decided to just simply put laws that would make movement by noncitizen citizens illegal. Her mom had gotten them fake papers for each of the three territories they would trek through with various identities. Amethyst didn't know when she did this, but she did notice their nice TV was gone along with most of the jewelry her mom owned but never wore out. She used to tell Amethyst she'd get some of it when she turned twelve; then it was pushed to eighteen and again to when she was married and finally when she had a kid of her own. She guessed, in a way, she had gotten her inheritance early.

It was comforting just not having to worry about TerraTech (TT) to the same degree. Floating around were stories of students being taken from class, led to the nurses' station, and tested for the mutated gene by TerraTech officials. Their identities were then tagged in the national citizen database. It was the only way to know who was biologically Crow as the information wasn't kept track of. Those were the only citizen noncitizens they were concerned about. The kicker was no one was entirely sure how many there were, and over 4,000 was the best estimate. The exact number was believed to be around 4,735. An exact number was hard to pinpoint because some were shuffled around as kids to other families after the adoption process was finalized.

The entrance was right next to them as her mom decided to go around the back. In her stomach, she could feel the pain subsiding as if it knew she was about to eat. She didn't think about what she would eat or even if she wanted a burger in the first place, but the idea of something warm in the pit of her stomach sounded like the remedy to some of the pain. The building looked like a double-wide camping trailer with large bolted-on signs declaring the place Ricky's Burger Joint. The bright teal font was faded from the sun. Inside, there was only standing area and only one table in the corner, where there were, Amethyst assumed, a girl and her father eating their burgers with a side of fried pickles. She ordered a burger and fried pickles to go, wanting to sit in the back of the car and lie down while eating her food and letting the cool afternoon air go over her body. She knew this probably wouldn't happen until the food was cold, but it was nice to imagine.

Her mom didn't expect her back so soon, and she was listening to what news channels she could get. "It is Wednesday, March 14, 2074, and thirty-seven degrees Celsius. Pres. Luke Talis has halted negotiations with the energy company Rising Star so he could instead focus his energy on the influx of relocated Crow-born children and developing programs to reacclimatize them to the culture of the territory. The estimate of over 4,700 now has to account for the 1,100 who have been sent back."

"The drought that is facing the Robin Territory is now entering its one-hundredth day."

"Five Bluebird Territory students will fly to the United States to compete in an international spelling bee."

Amethyst hoped to hear more information about the protest in Ivy Ladder, but the signal they were receiving faded, and now they could only get a clear connection to the local highway channel. In this part of the country, people were talking about normal things like the weather and sports in fifteen-minute intervals. She couldn't remember the last time she heard a news story about simple subjects like weather or traffic and not twenty-four-hour coverage about floors of apartment complexes being empty and supermarkets not being able to keep up with citizens stocking up on food and batteries so they could flee.

Her mom didn't let them stock up because she said it would be too obvious that they were running. They didn't even pack large suitcases but totes with mostly their technology and paperwork and money. She packed her last school transcript in the off chance that she would be able to go back to school and actually finish. Her mom had filled the trunk a few days before they left with blankets, flashlights, nonperishable food, and a first aid kit. Her mom didn't know that she knew this, but she knew she had a gun.

Amethyst knew she should give her mom more credit but the idea of a gun in the car seemed like such a stupid thing to do in the first place.

She split her burger with her mom, who chewed as she scanned the map that lay over the dashboard. Amethyst didn't eat her half. They had a thick stretch of dark green terrain to get through before they even saw some semblance of civilization. They were avoiding the smaller towns, where they might stick out to locals. Amethyst had been dying for a nice coffee for over a week. The last coffee she had was instant from a gas station.

The only other time she saw her mom this focused on anything was when she was looking over the furniture catalog for the apartment. Her dad wasn't even as obsessed as her mom was, and he was an architect. Her mom compared every finish and fabric against one another and even used tools online to see what it would look like with the sun reflecting off it or the moon. Frankly, she found the entirely of it ridiculous, but it was nice to see her mom so happy.

When they weren't driving and things were quiet, she thought about Sasha and what he was doing in that moment. His family wasn't on the run, but Sasha was, for the most part, in an entirely different world from his dad. His dad was a major head researcher for TerraTech in their domestic technology division, and the easiest way for one to explain what they were and what they did was really to tell you what they didn't do. The skinny on it was that when they were formed, they found novel ways to use the rare species of animals and plants in medicine. They also handled security for top officials.

Sasha was involved in the Lost Children in a less dangerous way. He didn't do anything that could get him thrown into jail. He avoided going to school, but he was very active in all the anti-Crow-war forums. Amethyst used it for a time, but the more she was away from it, the less it made sense. It was like they spoke in code, like *Tt con-v on Wilkes* and other walls of text she didn't remember. It started out as a way for her and her classmates to air out their grievances and call papers out on their outright lies about what the "children" like themselves wanted out of the negotiations, and it just became a dark place.

A month or so before they left, there was an article published at school that stated the number of children at 4,735 and that, because of missing files, that number may grow. The article continued at the very back of the paper with the known names. Rachel York published the article at school, and a bigger paper simply lifted the names. Shortly after her article was published, she left school. No one was certain why she did this. She wasn't an outcast. People liked her. Everyone knew her since her first year.

Amethyst's mom turned the car back on and began rolling her napkin on her jeans before tossing it into a plastic bag she kept on the passenger side. Amethyst pulled the cotton blanket up to her cheeks and tried to stay still to keep the stomach pain at bay. The soft snap of damp twigs reached her ears as they pulled out of the burger joint's lot, and they were on their way toward Amaryllis, the first instance they would be crossing any territory's border. On this leg of the journey, Amethyst would be Sarah Vaughn. It was ridiculous to her that anyone would think this tan-complected, dark-haired, and brown-eyed teenager was a Sarah, but as long as she said it convincingly, she guessed it didn't matter.

Her mom was drinking coffee when Amethyst woke up. The radio was softly playing news, weather, and traffic report that looped every fifteen minutes. The loudest sound was the segment's theme audio. Arnett turned her head slightly, with the air playing across the top of her head twisting up the brown bob like a crown. "There's a bagel in that bag."

"Five dozen protest signs have been removed from the gate at the city hall after complaints by citizens . . ."

"An accident involving multiple cars and a tow truck on the Burly Loop has stopped traffic for more than five hours. Emergency services are finding it difficult to clear the road of debris . . ."

"Good morning." Amethyst uncoiled her body from around the blanket and grabbed the bag on the floorboard. She was logging out of the GPS and downloading new maps, the satellite connection finally strong enough. They wouldn't have to depend on a paper map anymore. "This area smells like farm. How much longer until we're out of it?"

"Amie, most of the territories smell like farm—well, shit, I suppose."

"I don't think I can eat this right now. Can I have some coffee?" Her hand hovered over the cup holder, and her mom nodded.

"We'll have to get you some new clothes. I'm adding another rule: no wearing the same thing at every stop. You'll change in the car." Her mom added more maps to the queue to be downloaded.

Amethyst didn't know why it just sank her. The rule of mostly stopping at major cities was hard enough, almost as hard as the rule to not talk about Sasha, but keeping track of everything she wore and changing in the car added to the long list of things she already would forget. She had a closet full of clothes at home, but she usually wore four pieces: leggings, a Lake Placid T-shirt, a Sherpa hoodie, and a jean skirt she'd sometimes wear over the leggings. She didn't see herself as imaginative.

In the middle of her thoughts, she almost didn't see the skyscraper coming into view. It looked like a gently pulled bow or a sailboat wading through lush greenery. She couldn't see anything but it and the trees until much later. The farther they drove, the closer together cop cars became. The Grasshopper police cruisers were a deep emerald green, almost camouflaged against moss-carpeted woods like bejeweled beetles. Some had only their lights on. Every few moments, a stream of white and green light from the blinkers of the green and white cruisers would fill the car and reflect off the many screens on the dash. Her mom kept driving.

The cruelly shiny border sign was in full view ahead of them, but they were stuck behind a long line of cars. Her mom pulled out the fake papers and put them into the cup holder. She must have adjusted her seat belt half a dozen times. Amethyst moved to the front seat, poised and ready to answer and add to any questions her mom would be asked. The officers wore wide-brimmed emerald hats and tall black boots over riding breeches. A hand would stick out; the officer spent a millisecond inspecting before scanning and handing it back.

Amethyst took out one of the passports and looked for something that looked like a barcode.

"It's the seal, Amethyst. The seal is where they scan."

"Oh," Amethyst felt foolish in the moment.

"Have a little more faith in me." Her mom chuckled, still holding the steering wheel at a perfect ten and two. They were next in line, and the progression suddenly stopped. The scanner that looked like a silver price gun seemed to be broken. The officer hit it with his open palm a couple of times; then he tried it again and then his partner's scanner. His partner was a woman, and as he further inspected the document, she asked for more forms of identification. The man obliged, handing over a finger-thick stack of paper in one wide arm sweep. He didn't look through it but instead slid his finger over it like a flip-book and handed it back. They were waved forward. Her mom drove a little too fast and stopped with a sharp lurch forward. She could hear the stress on the tires.

"Good afternoon . . . good afternoon, lady," the officer said to Amethyst, slightly leaning into the window.

Amethyst smiled and waved. His eyes were almost black, like tiny lead balls. His lopsided smile was a tight line.

He pointed to the GPS. "Haven't seen one of those in a while."

"Just gonna drive it until the wheels fall off." She slapped her hand against the steering wheel, nearly missing.

The officer nodded and held out his hand. As he inspected the papers, Amethyst saw his eyebrow lift.

"These are new. When did you both relocate?"

"A few weeks ago. This one wants to go Merriweather University, early admittance."

Amethyst nodded. She didn't want to go to that granola school.

"My daughter goes there now. She's in her second year. Far cheaper than some of the other territory schools. Maykis is robbery." He took off his hat, his black hair slicked against his head from the sweat.

Maykis is a hundred times better, Amethyst thought. The top schools were Talis University, Maykis University and Kroft Technical, all three were founded by the most powerful families in all the unified and unified territories. To gain admittance was like securing a higher rank for your family name.

He scanned both of the passports and handed them back to her mom. She put them in the cup holder and slowly pulled forward before steadily picking up speed five miles over the already high speed limit.

"You did really well. He seemed to believe you." Amethyst's mom took out a hard candy from the glove box and put it in her mouth, taking off the wrapper in one pull after. She always found that gross, but how does one tell their own mother that? She tossed the wrapper on the floorboard and turned the GPS, flipping to only the second out of our many queue maps. "So I have a whole backstory?"

"Well, fragmented pieces and such. You're eighteen. I added a few extra months, and you're looking at colleges. I just made the Merriweather part up then and there. No one is gonna think it's odd that a girl of your age is traveling all over to look at colleges during spring break. Just when we get to the ununified territories, let me do most of the talking." Amethyst hated the entire situation. She would rather be studying for exams and doing anything else but running. Running was always the idea her mom floated to when things became less tame in the territory. The only reason she relented was because once she was in Arestromer she could see if this Doctor Miles was all he was cracked up to be. On the boards she was on for Lost Children, he was mentioned practically weekly for helping those who had the illness, Who the hell knew if he had a cure but if he had something that reduced the frequency of it, she would gladly take it.

The sun had set, and the beam of the headlights crested out ahead of the pair, transforming the black asphalt into a winding, never-ending island. The trees seemed to recede further into the background. The ununified territories was a snide and shorthand way of saying a group of countries totally uninterested in participating in the long history of violence the unified territories inflicted on one another.

Maykis Isle was the one exception. It was less of a country and more of a gigantic campus for TerraTech, the world's largest technology and agriculture company. If you had a communicator, was prescribed anything, and had food on your table, TerraTech had a hand in it.

The road became narrow as they made a smooth turn around a gently sloping hill. A few houses sat at the top. The only evident way up to them was thick concrete stairs illuminated by rods of light below each step. In that moment, Amethyst would have loved to be supine underneath a fluffy white comforter on an actual bed. She wondered what they were sitting down to eat and what they were talking about at the kitchen table.

Amethyst couldn't remember the last conversation she had at the dinner table with her dad. She only remembers she didn't sleep well that night.

"When we reach the city limits, we'll stay in a hotel. If I make good time, we should have six, maybe seven hours to spare." Her mom seemed to be counting the invisible hours on her fingertips as she tapped them on the steering wheel.

"Don't worry about it," Amethyst really meant it. To take further time away from the trip meant to prolong her getting any help.

"No, no. We're going to stay in a hotel," Her mom shook her head indicating that the decision was final.

Amethyst moved to the back seat, looking into the back window, watching the white dashes stretch and pull themselves out from under them, her blanket still in a coil at the center. "What's my name?"

"It's Lina Bard right now."

"Hmm, did Dad come up with it?"

"Yeah, he did." Her voice was softer.

❧

When Amethyst closed her eyes, she can still sense within her the presence of her room, feeling like she was still sitting on her own bed underneath the sloping ceiling and the vibe of her stuff around her playing on her skin. She could smell the slightly damp air, rotting wood, and the old-smelling tapestry that hung next to the armoire. There was no ceremony when she left. Her mom asked if she wanted coffee, and she quickly went to the bathroom, grabbed her wristlet, and left. When she got into the car and saw the back filled with totes, she said nothing as they drove past the coffee shop. It took everything in her soul not to cry that day. To cry would be to bust the plan wide open and be caught.

There were piles of powdered glass in the street from last night's sonic explosion by TerraTech, along with flattened soda cans and bottles, trampled protest signs, and evidence of small fires. It wasn't a long protest. When the crowd grew to a width of two streets, the warning siren began to bleat, the windows spewed glass like dust, and they ran. Amethyst was too tired to watch the news that night. It had been nearly three years since this all started. It didn't start with a bang. People didn't get angry right away. First there were whispers about the news and people who weren't on either side, just merely ambivalent. Then there were her classmates, broken-hearted who continued to do as they were told. They floated from day to day too sad to do anything else. And when one would expect acceptance of what was happening, rumbles started to quake below the surface.

The next city they would enter was Amaryllis. It was built partially on the side of the Cedar Mountains before the range split, revealing the bay. Bluebirds often got married there. Her mom and dad got married at the courthouse a few blocks from where they lived but had a ceremony there. Amethyst was turning over a jawbreaker in her mouth as the landscape started to be pierced with bolts of steel and glass.

"Turn right on Dowling Road."

"About two hours, then a nice nap in bed, maybe a bath if they have one." Her mom glanced at the GPS.

"What's in the area?" Amethyst reached toward the cup holder for her hot bottle of water. Making conversation would be better than sitting there letting her mom guess at what she was thinking.

Her mom slid the map to the side, revealing a list of the closest attractions. "A mall is around the corner from the hotel. There's also a park and a water fountain. Maybe tonight we'll stretch our legs." There would be no way they could go to a mall.

At the mention of movement, she could feel her feet throb with anticipation. "The news?" Amethyst said, unintentionally speaking low.

"TerraTech is sending new weapons to officers in the Bluebird Territory. Doesn't say what they are or what they do. Oh god, is this maddening!" Her mom roughly swiped that headline across the screen: SHORTAGE ON PLASTIC. Another swipe—ROLLING BLACKOUTS IN THE CROW TERRITORY. She let the story disappear as it was again replaced with dockets of maps waiting to be used, each showing a small square of land.

"Sa"

Her mom held up her hand to shush her. "We shouldn't talk about him." She turned her head to the back of the SUV and looked past Amethyst's face and out the back seat window. Sasha was the last person she had back home that didn't change with everything that happened. He was still his puppy dog self. She couldn't just abandon him from her mind like that.

She ignored the warning as she only needed to say one thing. "He told me what they look like, what they do."

"When was this?"

"A few months before we left."

"Well, don't just sit on that information."

"It's like a radio waveno, more like a sonar. It disrupts thoughts and makes people faint." Amethyst put up her pointer fingers and spread them about eight inches apart. "The device is about this big. It looks like a gun, but it's really shiny. It looks like it's fake."

"Where did he see it?"

"In his dad's files."

"Are you sure about that? Do you realize what you're saying?"

Amethyst knew exactly what she was saying. Sasha's dad was behind a project that was going after people against the negotiations and sending the children (i.e., people like herself) back to their biological parents. She had processed the information often enough through her brain that she no longer internally shook, but instead, she sank deep down into herself, bracing for the inevitable. She had already let all the menacing images of what the thing could look like run through her mind. She was thankful for Sasha, thankful that he had not changed.

Her mom pulled the car over on the side of the road. The car came to a slow careen into thick mud. She took her cell phone out of the glove box and began texting, the faux typing noise an unending song of old-sounding clicks of a typewriter. She was probably texting Lucy about what she had said. She wanted to ask in that moment, but Amethyst didn't want to break her mom's train of thought.

She handed Amethyst her phone and started driving. "Talk to her if she texts back or calls. We're making good time."

The phone smelled like old ketchup from baking in the glove compartment in the hot sun. She had texted Lucy, "Text back as soon as possible." Lucy didn't text back, and Amethyst held the cell phone in her hands between her legs for the rest of the ride to the hotel.

"Do you need anything?" Her mom looked ahead, peeked at the map, and refocused.

"I don't think so. I mean, some more pillows for the car would be nice."

"Not too many though. We don't want anyone thinking we're living in the car. It might make people—"

"I know. I know, Mom." Amethyst was tired all the rules and tired of all the constant reminders.

"It's not that I don't want you to have it. I just want us to be careful." Her mom looked at the phone in Amethyst's lap.

"Nothing yet." Amethyst felt the anxiety creep up her spine. It made her body feel less reactive. Nearly frozen, and she could tell her mom was caught in this loop. She would look at the map, the road, and again the phone. The button was green, indicating that sound notifications were toggled on, yet her mom could not help herself but look.

Amethyst didn't have anywhere to look but the animated map on the GPS. Her mom had taken her phone before they left. Occasionally, Amethyst would take it to text Sasha or survey the boards about Doctor Miles, knowing she hid it in her suitcase inside a faux bar of soap, but she had to be careful to do this when her mom was in a deep sleep and there was no one else around. Amethyst didn't know why she didn't just destroy it, but she wasn't going to question it and get the one bright spot in her life taken away. Sasha didn't text back often, but a word was enough for Amethyst. It let her know that he was alive and that he was still himself. It did give her hope that her mom thought they were that close to freedom and normalcy that she could soon be left with her cell phone.

The Dyker Hotel was a two-story glass building curled around a large water fountain. Their room was the farthest back, and from the back hall window, they could see a dark green lawn before it sloped down to the highway. Across from them in the left corner was another group of rooms, and between that was a small courtyard with a square fountain. They would be sharing the bed, but the first thing Amethyst's mom did was open the paper map and take off her shoes as soon as Amethyst opened the room door.

Her mom spoke toward the map. "Draw the blinds."

Amethyst drew the blinds and then took her pants before scooting herself up on the white comforter. "No text yet," she said, looking at the shape of the phone in her pants pocket on the floor.

"She could still be driving. Takes a while to get from Bell Whispers to here."

Bell Whispers was in the middle of the Robin Territory on the left.

Lucy was Arnett's friend from college. When this tougher effort to send Lost Children began a year ago, they reconnected. Lucy was one of the first to state it could start a war. They traded information about what the Crow government was up to nearly every day and sometimes all night, just walls of text in rapid succession. Lucy helped her mom prepare to leave without her even noticing it. She was a treasure of a person in her mom's eyes.

Amethyst did not remember falling asleep, but when she popped up, it was as if she pulled herself out of a casket like Dracula. Her mom was lying next to her, with the map and a few thin markers at the foot of the bed. There were beginnings of daylight, and the soft white orbs of light beside each door were turning on one by one. Her mom was snoring into her pillow. She went to check the phone for a text and saw there was a recorded message. She clicked on the play button and put it to her ear.

"I don't know where you are exactly, but there are more checkpoints now. I'm nowhere near Bell Whispers. Call me so we can discuss plan B. They're not letting anyone out of Maykis Isle. I'll need to get some help from some talented friends. Do you have the numbers I gave you? Don't text, OK? Don't text. Don't. Just record a message."

Amethyst woke up her mom immediately. Her mom rubbed her face in the pillow before mouthing "what?" with her eyes still closed. Her mom listened to the message, walking to the bedroom as Lucy's voice became more panicked. In her head, Amethyst could not help picturing her Lucy on the side of the road, recording the message, looking at the long stretch of cars along the highway, with the Authority directing the traffic across the strip of grass so they could go back. Her mom slid on her boots. "I'm gonna need a lot of privacy for this. Be ready to leave in a few minutes."

"OK."

Her mom quickly went to the bathroom, and Amethyst could hear a flutter of typing that lasted a nanosecond before she turned on the sink.

She didn't hear the recorded message as her mom had her wait in the car for her on the side of the road, not exactly a safe place for a teenager to be at 4:29 a.m., but she knew it was to keep her safe in other ways. Later that morning, she bought Amethyst coffee from an actual coffeehouse and not at a gas station. She was somewhat annoyed because she woke her up, and she wanted to enjoy sleeping for at least another hour, tricking her mind into thinking she was still in the hotel's queen-size bed and not in the back seat of an SUV.

Lucy still had not responded. As they headed toward one of Lucy's talented friends, the number of patrol cars thickened in the artery of the downtown freeway. All the people in the cars looked normal, like they were off to do normal things like go to work or school or kill time in a convenience store parking lot.

"Do you think they know what's going on? Like, really know?"

"The human mind has a knack for protecting itself." Her mom shook her head, almost in agreement with herself.

Running often didn't feel like running. It felt like standing in plain sight, waiting for something to happen. You'd think there would be a rush, some kind of adrenaline pumping, but it was all anxiety. It was all quiet. Most of the time, her mom was silent; and when she wasn't, she was telling her what she should do. She just followed directions, and beyond that, not much went through her mind.

The talented friend met Amethyst' mom in the parking lot of a mall. He was a tall man with hair down to his behind. He wore navy slacks and a white button-down. His left forearm had one large porcelain-white splotch. Amethyst couldn't hear his voice from where she was standing, but his laugh made her want to laugh, and she had no idea what they were talking about.

She got to stretch her legs but only as far as the other end of the lot and in her mom's line of sight. The lot wasn't empty. The shopping cart return areas were mostly empty. Kids were being unloaded and reloaded into SUVs, and families were packing their trunks with groceries in cardboard boxes. One little girl was being wheeled around in a shopping cart toward a white car by whom Amethyst assumed was her dad. She held on to a box of fruit snacks or bribe as her mom would call it. There was a duck pond, and every few moments, there would be a stiff breeze that smelled of mowed grass and manure. She walked through each row of cars as if she was trying to find her own.

Her mom waved her over as she was about to turn down another section. The man's name was Joshua. He had a thick French accent. "I wanted to see who was the reason for all this! How are you, my dear?"

"I'm here." She didn't mean for it to sound as ungrateful as it did, but she hadn't had a good night's sleep consistently for a while.

Her mom's entire disposition had changed, and she was beaming at the man. She leaned in and whispered in her ear, "He's found us an easy way out of here. We're going there now."

She didn't even know what this plan entailed, but from her mom's mood, she was excited herself. She and her mom walked back to the car, and they followed his compact red car for a few miles before turning into a local road. They both parked in a large cobblestone driveway before they followed him up a sloping hill and down a trail. Amethyst made sure to take her cell phone out of the tote and conceal it in her underwear. A few cyclists passed them. A short-haired blond woman on a blue bike waved and smiled.

Joshua led them to a wooden door tucked into the side of a hill. It would have looked like something out of a fantasy novel if there wasn't a clearly man-made stream beside it. A large orange pipe drained into the left side, and it didn't look all that fresh. Some areas seemed to be frothy and stagnant.

A stiff breeze of refrigerated air filled Amethyst's nose as the door was opened. She expected to see a cutout of a tree or some other indication that the room was formed from a tree, but there was only cold concrete. He led them down a long hall and to another much heavier door kept closed with a large red padlock. The sound of the water rushing through the ground beneath them was so steady that it was drone-like.

Pain

Sasha: October 5, 2073

The dust from the windowsill floated on the midmorning shafts of light. Sasha remembered turning over in the night when the pain was a dull ache in the pit of his stomach. Now the pain was like an earthquake compared with the dull roar it used to be.

His throat felt parched from panting all night. His brow was drenched in sweat. He knew he had to call out to someone, but he didn't know who he should choose. He felt he only had enough energy to call out to one person. It would either be his dad or his bodyguard.

Another wave overtook him, threatening to knock all the air out of his lungs. It stuck around for a few moments before feeling as though it was seeping down the pit of his stomach to his feet. Sasha breathed. These episodes had recently become more common. This was his third this month and his fifth in the last six months. He didn't know if he could keep up with the pain. His whole being felt like it was twisted up. Cold—he felt cold too.

On his nightstand, he could see the water he had poured last night when he thought the ache was from lack of water. The pain slammed into him again as if to dismiss his earlier foolish thought.

"Dad." His voice was strained, suffocated by the pain he bit back down his throat. He wouldn't be able to hear him unless he screamed. He didn't have the energy. His energy was reserved for keeping himself focused enough not to get swept away.

Someone would notice he was sleeping in and get him. There was no way that he would have to lay here for too long. It was a Tuesday morning, and he should be in class.

Sasha tried to focus on something else. He looked around the room and saw the curlicue pattern on the Bluebird Territory tapestry Rita had made for him. Around the edge rose hips forming their own frame, and more towards the center a perched Eastern Bluebird. He studied the loops of the curlicue pattern. The vibrant blue they were made of made his eyes ache. He closed his eyes and groaned through yet another wave. The slight shift he made on his bed made him aware of the dampness on his back. It had never been this bad before.

The first time this had happened was two years ago. He was thankfully home when it hit because the pain brought him to his knees. His dad rushed him to the emergency room, where some of his classmates were experiencing a similar pain. It wasn't his appendix like they initially thought. Nothing appeared to be wrong, but the pain continued to come back. It stopped for a while, and now it seemed as though it was making up for lost time.

A moment later, he heard the sound of keys clinking in the key bowl. He sucked in the cold air of the room and let out another grunt that was just a one octave higher. Steady steps were headed toward his room now, which was on the far end of the house in the turret.

"Dad," Sasha managed.

His dad opened the room door and walked over to Sasha. Confusion marred his features. "How long have you been like this? Breathe, Sasha!"

"All night." His voice was barely a whisper.

❧

Dr. Price came over within forty minutes. Sasha was on the edge of fainting by that point, his breathing labored and his face red. The morphine was slow to touch the pain. His dad pushed water on him once he was able to freely move without pain. The water hurt Sasha's strained throat. Dr. Price got another call, so she left shortly after coming. She promised to come back later in the evening just in case the pain had come back.

"You want to sit up more?"

"Yeah." Sasha nodded.

His dad was sitting next to him on the bed, guiding him up by his back.

❧

A few moments later, Sasha could hear his dad on the phone with the school, letting them know that he would be absent tomorrow. The pain was gone, but the ghost of it was still slipped over his body like a glove. His entire body ached. He swung his legs down from the bed and let his feet touch the cold floor. It hurt to have any weight on his legs. He let the heels of his feet slightly hover above the floor so as not to put any weight on them. When he gathered up enough courage, he walked over to the kitchen to attempt to eat, the pit of his stomach an empty expanse.

There was leftover pizza at the back of the fridge from last night. He ate it at the kitchen island cold, finding the act of raising his arms above his head to microwave the slice a painful act.

His dad had pricked his finger before leaving again for the lab in Bluebird Stream proper. Sasha already knew he was a Lost Child or rather one of the relocated child of some Crow family who thought he would be better off in the Bluebird Territory. He didn't know what his dad was trying to find now, but he wished he didn't have to be prodded anymore. It wasn't typically painful, but with his soreness, it radiated up his arm.

❧

"October 8, 2073," the findings report read at the top. A half-green and half-yellow bar at the top of the page showed the scale at which gene 8alpha6 was barely registering. His dad hovered over him as he looked at the report himself. There was no talk about what it could mean, but his dad's disposition had changed.

"Whatever it was or is, it appears to be leaving your system."

Sasha didn't say anything, and he wasn't even brave enough to consider the possibility that the pain would end out of fear of great disappointment when the pain resurfaced.

QUIET

Amethyst

A *couple days ago*

The TV was on in the background, a commercial playing now and Amethyst's mom was in the kitchen making breakfast. This wasn't a normal occurrence. She typically didn't make breakfast unless it was a special day. There was something lighter about how she carried herself that morning, but Amethyst couldn't place how or why. In front of Amethyst was her project for cultural studies. It was the project that every senior dreaded. It was essentially a rehashing of all that made the planned country of Cadril unique. First was the obvious, each of the seven territories being named after birds or insects, either fantasy like the Phoenix or real like Bluebird, Crow, Robin, Eagle, Raven or Grasshopper. Next it was things like the names for the different types of mask and their color names. It wasn't green but, emerald and it wasn't red but vermillion. Her mom didn't pressure her like she usually did to finish the project, so Amethyst lacked the focus to do so.

In the middle of the night Amethyst could hear her mom rustling some things about in the garage. She knew it was her because she could hear the shuffling steps of her slippers. Unable to sleep she left her room and decided to head to the bathroom. The bathroom looked stripped bare of most of the essentials and neither of their toothbrushes were there. She decided to get dress, the action completed almost robotically and headed down toward the garage that was just below them. On her way down in the elevator she ran into her neighbor Rita. She was a local artisan who sometimes would get commissions from families like Sasha's. The garage was part parking and part storage. On the right were cars and on the left were big metal cages where people would store their bikes and out of season equipment like bats and skis. Her mom was down there. She was putting a yellow and black plastic tote into the trunk.

"Get in Amethyst. I have your cell. Just in."

It felt like all the air in the garage had been sucked out with a straw and she could almost feel herself loose the rigidity her body once had. She said nothing back and opened the passenger door. In the cupholder was a bottle of water and their toothbrushes. Just moments later they were on the road. The early phases of daylight were glowing before them.

Amethyst remembered she left the bathroom light on and worried about it for a moment until she realized that they automatically shut off after a few hours. They stopped for coffee at a gas station and continued on their way. The two cups stayed untouched for the better part of the morning. Nothing was said until her mom started to cue up maps for them. The first being one that would take them to Moss Point. They had a while to go because Bluebird Stream was a good twelve hours away.

"Are you going to drink your coffee?"

"No, I don't know why I stopped. I really shouldn't have done that."

"We're—

She couldn't finish the sentence. She should have known but there was something in her mind protecting her from completing the thought. It was something she had always heard about people doing and her mom would mention it in passing but she did not realize her mom actually had the nerve in her to run. Her heart felt more like a ball of flesh in her chest cavity, suffocatingly so.

"We're going to Moss Point, we'll stay somewhere…and then Amaryllis…and then Somber. We just have to cross into Arestromer."

Her mom didn't need to explain it any further. It was the same story. Lost Children would go to Arestromer because the laws didn't apply to that part of the non-unified territories and essentially wait it out was all that could be done. Arestromer wasn't this lavish territory. It was most small towns and farms. A lot of the people there fished as well. The beaches were the most incredible part. The northern part was white sandy beaches from one end to the other. Amethyst doubted they'd ever see the beaches, but it didn't hurt to dream.

She floated back and forth between the thought she didn't want to run, and she felt lighter as everything she had ever known was rushing past her. The bookstore where she bought her new fitted mask for graduation, the café were she would spend entirely too much time and the animal rescue mission where she would cuddle the dogs. When they passed by the school, she remembered her project sitting unfinished on the coffee table.

Corn Silk

Sasha

"It's like always wearing earmuffs—no, better yet, having your head stuck in a plexiglass cube."

"You're being dramatic."

"No, really, the closest thing I can hear is the blood whooshing through my ears. Anything beyond that is muffled." He clasped his ears with his hands and widened his eyes for emphasis.

The floor of the café was dusted here and there with tiny bits of glass trampled in by people. Yesterday afternoon, there was a protest against TerraTech. TerraTech didn't like it so a big *boom* The windows of nearly every store on Manor Street seized and then popped like a bag of flour, pouring powdered glass into the street. Places like the café and the big mall on the corner were fine. TerraTech outfitted the stores with industrial-grade TerraTech glass. Sasha wasn't there, but his bedroom was right above the café, and he found himself, in the next moment, momentarily deaf. Muse was on the street and said she can hear just fine now. But that was February 22nd, and it was already the 28th.

"Sasha, maybe go to a doctor?" Muse drank the last bit of coffee in her mug, sat it on the plate, and patted his hand and in that gesture was saying, *You worry too much, and thank you for the coffee.*

❧

Later that night, he tried again to text Amethyst. She became a runner. Her mom was smart, though, because even he didn't suspect she was leaving. Most people went to Arestromer because it was not unified with the other territories. But he had no idea. Maybe she was even more desperate and went to America.

Living in the Bluebird Territory was like being center stage. Everyone was watching the drama and action, but no one was doing anything. They sent their news cameras to watch but did nothing when the state-sanctioned terrorist TerraTech made students deaf or wasted hundreds of thousands of gallons of water because of an "accidental" error, strangely enough, in the one area where the most protesters lived, and he was sick of it.

He got a "hi" from her at 10:41 p.m. and then an "are u up" that he'd missed because he met with Muse to finish her art. His hands were still dry and raw from the last batch of corn husk dolls they twisted together. He offered to make it faster for her by just tying them together in twine to give the suggestion of a fully formed corn husk doll, but she said, "No. Help, or don't help." They met in the back of her apartment complex and sat cross-legged in the parking lot, surrounded by dried husk and corn silk. She put on music from her phone, '90s music playing from the top forty.

"Amethyst text back?"

"Nope. That's fifty." Sasha tossed another little body onto the pile.

"Just another ten." She folded another large strip of corn husk over in half to start a new one.

"How many people are coming?"

"A couple, maybe no one. It doesn't matter. I'll film it." Muse had developed a grove and finished the majority of the last ones and simply shooed Sasha away.

❧

His dad was still on TerraTech campus because, from his phone, he got a ping that he just bought lunch on campus. Sasha didn't know if he knew he still got the notifications. He may be in tech, but he was still old.

Sasha rolled over on his bed and set his phone on the nightstand. Monday the 5th Muse would line up thousands of the dolls she made around the Maykis statue. He didn't know what it meant. He knew the number of Lost Children. Everyone did at this point, but why corn husk, and why at the foot of the Maykis statue? Muse tried to explain it to him, but then she got frustrated and just started to mess around on her phone.

When he saw the text the next morning, he texted back, asking how she felt. Now to her, it would be a small nugget of inconsequential information she wouldn't feel guilty about sharing; but for him, it would slowly tell him where she was in the process. He could relay that information to his dad, and they could figure out when she left and how much time she had until the gene could potentially be suppressed. She had five bouts of pain in the last month, and that was how it began for Sasha before it ended for him last year. Amethyst could change very soon. If they didn't catch up to her, she could also die instead. They couldn't have that happen before she was back with her birth parents.

Sasha met up with Muse at the statue. He wasn't expecting many people to show up because Muse was more of an interesting artist rather than a talented one. But wrapped around the base of the acid-rain-faded bronze galloping horse were crowds of shouting people. Their faces were decorated in blue lattice designs from their cheeks to their collarbones. They called themselves the Blue Lattice Network. They made sure to protect as many people as they could during protest. The designs were pretty; in the middle of the smog of the city center and mud and leftover slush from the torrential snow they got a few days ago, there was the deepest concentration of Persian blue. The curlicue design was delicately surrounded by a small floral design that danced around the curving lines.

This would go like these always went. The crowd would swell in size, spilling onto the sidewalk, and slowly become big enough to start choking up traffic and loud enough that regular people would start to take notice, and once the decibel level was maintained for a solid two minutes, Terra-Tech would do its thing. Sasha was guessing sirens this time.

"Almost time." Muse smiled and dug her right hand into her mustard-colored cords intertwined in hair. Sasha was sure this was it. There had to had been about a hundred people gathered and shouting, "Leave our children be!" and "Blue forever!" And the nearly five thousand little corn husk dolls were covered from the splatter of dirty snow by people passing.

Muse took out a lighter from her pocket, balancing her cell in her hand to record the act, and before Sasha could grab her arm to stop her, he saw the lighter drop between the third and fourth rows of dolls, and the fire burst and fanned onto row after row. Most of them were black and falling to pieces before he could register what had happened. The crowd liked it.

The pitch rose, and any order there was taken away. He reflexively grabbed Muse by the arm and pulled her away from the fire. He picked up her cell phone from the flames and put it in his back pocket. Setting fire to things was a crime, and Sasha guessed or perhaps he just always assumed Muse knew that.

The fire started to create a cloud of soot and ash, and far away, he could hear fire trucks approaching. Muse didn't want to go, and she turned back toward the fire. Sasha could feel the buzzing of the TerraTech app notification on his phone. It would be mere moments before something bad happened, something strong enough to dissipate the crowd, and it was a big crowd. He pulled her again, and she nearly tripped over her own feet as he led her across the street and into the park. The siren started, loud enough to make anything anyone said inaudible. But then puffs of smoke drifted from a large curlicue circle gate at the base of the lamppost. That could only be pepper spray. He continued to pull her until her mind caught up with his, and she was running on her own. The sirens began blaring in a rhythmic fashion, and in between each wail, Sasha could hear the sound of shouting and running and some crying.

"What . . . is . . . happening?" Muse catapulted her voice to each word.

"Terra . . . Tech."

If she hadn't started an actual fire, it would not have been so bad. It would have been just sirens or ice-cold air that poured out from every vent available at the storefronts TerraTech rented. He needed to let his dad know who she was so she'd be just watched and not arrested. Sasha liked Muse.

The ground was now covered in glass, more dead leaves, and some other debris from the trees. There was red dye that began to spray into the streets from the storefronts, marking everyone who passed through. It was a marker for police. Anyone covered in red would be questioned. He hoped they wouldn't use the dye. Dye usually meant that with arrest would come testing for the mutated gene, and those who were tested might disappear.

The disappearing was a new development. Usually, people were tested and left alone, but the Crow government was becoming less trusting that the Bluebird Territory would actually return the Lost Children and were taking matters into their own hands. Sasha would be safe, but Muse and their classmates would not be safe. He had to get her out of the city square as fast as possible.

Sirens started to bleat in a new rhythm. It was a warning that police were coming. Cars began to appear from up the road, near the bottling plant, creating a sea of sharp white and blue light converging on the city square. Red dye was beginning to float from the light post in the park. The stuff was everywhere. In the middle of the red misty dye was concentrated sprays of marking dye. Some was already on Sasha and Muse. It was faint, but the more he walked through the park, it was guaranteed to get darker.

"Can you walk? Can you walk?" Sasha pulled her forward.

"Yes. Yes, I can walk. Stop pulling me. I'm OK." Muse shook her head like she disagreed with everything she had just said.

Sasha pulled her into his arms and toward the Tol Mountain replica in the middle of the park. Far off, he could hear shouting. Muse walked backward into the statue, stunned.

"Can you hear and see me all right?" Sasha looked intently into her eyes.

Muse nodded but didn't look straight. She looked dizzy. Sasha hoped whatever was wrong with her focus wasn't permanent.

"I want you to follow my fingers. Look up, please." Sasha moved his finger up and down and side to side.

Muse couldn't track his finger right away; her pupils were sluggishly going from one point to the next. "Where's my cell phone?"

Sasha touched his back pocket; it was gone. "I don't know. I had it. Hopefully, it's broken beyond all hope. Why would you record that?" Sasha was beginning to sound like the father in this relationship.

"We have to look for it! We don't know what happened to it. The Authority could have it!" Muse shook her head rapidly and then staggered back.

"We need to go somewhere safer. The park will soon be surrounded. Let's go out the back before the Authority starts searching the park." Sasha, out of habit, grabbed her arm and began to walk. Muse walked slowly at first but then quickly as the pitch of sirens increased. They went around the back of the apartment complex through the shared courtyard. Sasha let go of her when he saw two members of the Authority questioning a woman walking her dog. Both of them were men, wearing tall black boots and shirts with a perched heron that wrapped from their back to their shoulder. Sasha held Muse's hand instead. When they made it to the stairwell, Muse took a deep breath and began taking a slow ascent up the stairs.

"Apartment six," Sasha called ahead.

She had made it back to his apartment with only some cuts, a bruised left foot from twisting it on the curb, and red-tinged eyes. Sasha took some pictures for her doctor for her because her phone was still MIA. The location app couldn't locate the phone, but this turned out to be a boon for Sasha. He needed to take pictures of her for his dad's for the database. Only phones with a microchip like his could communicate directly with TerraTech agents like his dad. He needed to know that Muse was part of his long game and not to send her to her birth parents right away.

Amethyst texted back right after he had sent his dad the pictures. It was like Christmas. When Muse left, Sasha texted her back. Amethyst said, "The pain is bad. I live in warm baths. The sky always seems lightly golden here." He then forwarded the text to his dad with no context and considered his work for the week done.

Later, Sasha got a call. He didn't answer it because he had company over, but she had left a voice mail. "Hey, are you guys OK? There's a video floating around of a fire. You guys were gassed. Please tell me you're not hurt. Don't . . . spare me or anything. TerraTech is trying to find whoever did it so they can arrest them. Don't do anything for a while, OK?"

She sounded like wherever she was, it was desolate. Sasha didn't even hear cars going by, maybe in the countryside. He filed the information away in his brain and went back to playing with the strands of Zora's hair that flowed over his pillow. She was a lot like Muse—smart, interesting but also stupid in some important ways. He let her sleep while he went to get coffee.

When he came back, she had already left. He drank both lattes and then started back to the drawing board or rather message board to find out when the next protest would be. TerraTech already knew about the boards and how to decode them. It wasn't a secret at all. The danger only began once a protest actually took place. Judekid$* and DarmerUL were the most reliable when it came to organizing a protest. Sasha didn't know who they were in real life. He could find out, but that wasn't his focus at the moment.

Sasha's phone began buzzing in his pocket like he had smuggled a hive. Over and over again was a notification his dad called. He didn't bother to leave a voice mail or even text, just call. He was angry. He knew it. Sasha texted, "Hi. Busy. What's up" and as if the notifications were going to jump out of the phone and slap him, five new ones appeared. He pressed on one, and the phone began to ring.

The call connected, but he heard nothing . . . nothing. And then finally, there was a deep, resigned sigh. "What the fuck were you doing, Sasha?"

He didn't yell. It was controlled. He was ready to carve him out like a pumpkin. "Setting fire to a historical monument. I get it, sends a powerful message to people like me, but how could you let yourself be filmed and seen running away with that tramp? You look too involved. You looked like a criminal."

There was a long pause that made him take his phone from his ear to make sure he wasn't disconnected, and then in an angry rush, he said, "Give me her address. I don't have time to go to the office and look her up. I'm arresting her myself."

"You can't do that. I'm making progress. I can still help. Look . . . look." He took his phone from his ear and sent him the nonviral part of the video—the inner circle of the protest, his classmates. "There are still so many cases I can help you build. Don't do anything yet. It will look bad. I look good—"

"*Good!*"

"To them. To them, Dad."

"If I see another video with you in the middle of it, you're coming back home. I have spent the last few hours thinking of a way to explain away your dumbassery. Keep better tabs on that girl."

Sasha didn't know if it was mostly the coffee or the verbal beatdown alone, but his heart started to pound, and for a split second, the ringing in his ears came back. Muse was a handful only recently. When this all began almost a year ago in the early part of 2073, it was easier to know what she was thinking. It would be lunch, and she would announce to their friend group that she wanted to splash blue paint on the TerraTech HQ in Bluebird Stream, and that was that. No real filter on what should be kept a secret because it was just, in general, a better idea to keep whatever illegal things you planned to do a secret forever, even after you did it. Muse didn't get that memo until very recently, which was bad news for him.

Sasha didn't want to go back home and be under constant surveillance. In his apartment, he could have lunch or not have lunch and do it alone and not under the scrutiny of someone his dad paid to watch him. In his apartment, he could have friends over without their faces being scanned and put into a database. That didn't affect him per se, but it was annoying to be asked about everyone. Not everyone was a threat to national security. Sometimes he just liked to get drunk in the company of others.

Zora texted him, "Hey, look at you." And of course, it was about *the* video.

He texted back, "Ha." And he went back to scanning the boards for a likely protest.

Sasha met up with Muse a week later, and the tension from what TT did was still fresh in her mind. Muse looked up to the security cam bolted to the edge of the Inklings Bookshop. It had the three thin red lines on the black carbon metal casing that was synonymous with TerraTech. Sasha didn't know if it was this cam that tipped off those at the HQ in the Robin Territory or the one at the men's suit shop, but it didn't matter. She stood, squared up with it like she was ready to fight. Her two long black braids intertwined with yellow thread swayed back and forth across her back as she studied the cam. In the week that they had not seen each other, Muse was angrier than Sasha had ever seen her.

"Come, come." He sounded like he was talking to a child. It was not his intended tone, but she came anyway, still looking slightly up toward her enemy. Sasha was waiting longer than he cared to get more information about the next demonstration. There wasn't a time in his life since he was seven and broke the radio in the garage where he could almost feel the walls quake with his dad's anger. He needed something to distract his boss.

Sasha needed more bodies. He didn't like having the life he had, but the more names he produced, the closer they came to fracturing the movement from the inside and perhaps even tracking down Amethyst. It had been a while since she texted him, and he was sure her mom saw to that. Sasha rolled the ball of lint in his pants pocket, guessing the size, and breathed in the smell of roasting coffee beans and the sound of tiny pieces of pulverized sidewalk dragged underneath sneakers. He was here for now and would worry about the bigger things later.

Muse sighed and fiddled with the ends of her braids that were twisted up with bright yellow thread, slowly unraveling the ends a little. "You know a lot about me, right?" Muse said. They sat across each other at the coffee shop.

"We've known each other for about a few years. I would say I know a fair amount." Sasha watched as Muse studied the front lawn of the city hall that was slowly dying from a late frost.

"You told me a while ago that your dad worked for TerraTech." Muse turned her head toward him and looked at Sasha in the eyes. She slowly nodded yes, and he nodded once quickly, unsure if she wanted that response.

"He's on the board," Sasha said, which wasn't a lie, but if he told her what else he did, she wouldn't trust him.

"He's the head of research, Cayden Sasha Ashford." She spit out each one of his names like a hex.

"Is your name even Muse?" Sasha stopped drinking, putting distance between them by sliding out his chair.

"It is. I told you that." She looked utterly confused. Slowly, Muse swiped a strand of hair behind both ears and then nodded. She remembered the news article quite well; why didn't he? "You're not ready for this conversation. I am not either. But I want you to know that half-truths are full lies to me. I don't need that bullshit in my life. Do you really care about any of this? Are you just trying to make Daddy mad or something? Because I actually care about what happens to people like me." Muse blinked back tears as she held her coffee in increasingly unsteady hands. "Your father is the reason my eyes are still sore and why my leg is still swollen."

"I didn't do that to you. You know that, right?" He felt like she punched him in the chest.

"But you knew it was a possibility."

"I did not tell you to burn the dolls, Muse."

"So now you're just gonna tell me how to protest."

"Yes—"

"What the fu—"

"Because I don't want you to get hurt. They've killed people younger than you. I don't want that. You don't know how much I do not want that."

Muse clasped her hands together in prayer and exhaled in a huff like she was blowing her nose. Sasha found it cute. "Listen. OK. Just try to hear where I'm coming from—"

"Oh, I hear you. No matter what I do or how long, what matters to you is who my dad is. Actions don't matter," he said in a rush. He couldn't calm down his breathing.

"No. I agree with you. Actions do matter. The fact that you didn't tell me your dad was one of the most high-ranking officials in TerraTech says a lot. You may not be like him. I mean, who would I be to say that? But you know enough about how evil he is that you tried to hide it."

"Thank you for the coffee, Muse. I have to get back," Sasha said as he started to walk away.

The last bus had already left by the time he made it to the ticket station. Muse lived right across the town in what was seen as the political district of the territory where all the officials lived in their mansions, and the spaces between the stops were huge. By the time he got down the hill, there were at least three more ahead he could discern dotted with light. It took nearly twenty minutes for him to walk back to his apartment building. He guessed he shouldn't have been surprised by what he saw when he got there, but at that moment, he was shocked and more than a little pissed.

His windows were busted out, the wind beating against the white curtains. *Traitor* was spray-painted on the sidewalk, and the large windows to the lobby were covered with a cartoonish likeness of him, not Muse's hand but the art he did recognize from the street. He could have easily found out who it was by asking some rando on the street, but he stopped himself. Muse would hate him for it. She would know he had a hand in it, and she would never forgive him. He deserved at least this.

Sasha dusted the floor near the windows with flour and began sweeping the glass. The whole thing took more than an hour and a half. He went back to the boards. All the posters were posting in Anon, which could only mean big upcoming plans.

>TTBOY put in his place

^You know who?

> We're not going to use his name. The important people know who he is.

>I hope he gets the message.

^He won't. I'm sure he looks himself up. Seems like the type.

^Save us the PITA of letting him know we don't want to see his face anymore. The nerve to pretend actually to care. Is he even one of us? Does anyone know?

^He's not

^He actually is. Squirrel told me.

>Pics or it didn't happen . . .

<photo1>

<photo2>

<photo3>

<photo4>

>How spoiled can you be to get a whole-ass apartment to yourself, and you're still in your 20s?

^Is that what you're focusing on? Really? He's really dangerous. Maybe even unhinged.

>There were no screws to begin with; sure, it's genetic. TTBOY's dad helped develop Cerplex, the drug they give to prisoners to make them "behave," but it just dopes them up.

^I'm sure this was fun and all, but what if people get arrested for this? He doesn't own the apartment complex or the sidewalk.

^Yeah, sure, true, but it's going to be a pain for that TerraTech-funded sanitation truck to scrub it and Daddy to pay for all the damage.

^That's if he's not disowned.

He wasn't. But on some level, he wished he was. The conversation he had to have with his dad soon would end terribly. He'd be back in his castle on the hill in Bluebird Stream under his constant surveillance not because of the cost of the damage but because he embarrassed him. He didn't think he really cared what he did with his time, just so long as he stayed out of the paper. This would end up in the paper. It might even be a larger spread than the last one. It was controversial, and to a journalist, that was delicious.

The castle was an interesting place. It wasn't an actual castle but an apartment complex made to look like one. The building was this large, menacing red-bricked building with four thick turrets. Sasha used to live in an apartment that took up the entire top floor. His room was in the far-left turret. It was always bathed in unending amounts of sunlight. Even in winter, the window seemed to pull every glimmer of light it could find and laser-point it right onto all his monitors and into his eyes. Amethyst liked his room. She said it must be what heaven looked like. It was only bright. He didn't entirely understand that girl.

He closed what he could of the windows and drew the curtains. He couldn't sleep. Sasha refreshed the Ulink app over and over again, watching the cascading wall of text bounce down, forming steps. He fell asleep at some point and woke up with his cell phone in his hand. Muse had called twenty times. It was an unbroken stream of text: "U up," "U up," "U up," and finally "I can't reach Zora."

Sasha got dressed and plowed upper body first into the chilly fall, hoping his legs would keep the pace. There were eggs now decorating the sidewalk.

Hell

Sasha: January 13, 2072

The scene before him didn't seem like real life. Amethyst laid there, eyes tightly shut and tears staining her cheeks as another wave overtook her. Sasha felt useless, and in the moment, he was useless. His dad wasn't picking up his phone, and neither was Hakeem. She needed something. She looked like she was about to pass out, and no matter what he said to get her through another wave, it really meant nothing. Just moments ago, they were watching a movie, and she was headed to the bathroom. She fell then, the pain pulling her to her knees. At first, Sasha didn't know what was happening. He thought she stubbed her toe; but when he saw the pearls of sweat starting to form, he knew what was happening.

Watching her be dragged back into the pain over and over and over again made his heart feel like it would suffocate him. He would let her squeeze his hands, and at first, she seemed to be able to let out some of the pain onto him, but she was getting weaker. Her screams had faded into shallow pants.

Sasha periodically checked his phone, hoping to see a call, a text, just something. Amethyst was suddenly quiet, and her breathing seemed to deepen.

"Amie?"

She nodded. Good, she could at least focus through some of the pain.

The episode seemed to end then and there because she took a full breath, and her body that was once stiff like the blade of a sword was now relaxed.

❧

Sasha found a heated throw under the couch and put it over Amethyst. As she laid there, he drew her a really hot bath. Sasha really couldn't tell, but she looked as if she had fallen asleep. He stood over her watching her.

"You might want to take a hot bath. If you don't, your body is gonna feel really sore tomorrow, like you ran a marathon."

"Give me a minute." Amethyst sighed.

❧

Amethyst took a bath and changed into her pajamas, green plaid drawstring bottoms, and a white T-shirt. She walked as though she would fall through the floor as she made her way to the couch. His dad and, by extension, his bodyguard, Hakeem, were on their way. When they knocked on the door, Amethyst had fallen asleep.

"How is she?" his dad asked in hushed tones.

"She fell asleep."

"I could get Dr. Price here if she's still in pain."

"It started as quickly as it stopped. You just missed the opportunity." Sasha could hear the anger in his tone.

ARCHERY

Sasha: September 1, 2070

Each of the four tables had a stack of files on it for each student in the class as it would be just like last year and the year before that. Sasha stood behind a group of girls who were exchanging pictures on their phones. Closest to him was a short black-haired girl. Her hair hung below her butt in waves. Every few sections of hair were blue strands of embroidery floss wrapped tightly around it. The wavy-haired girl didn't say much.

The girl didn't appear to be a part of the group in front of her. Sasha had never seen someone so vibrantly dressed, even while in uniform. Instead of the required cream button-down blouse, she wore a frilly eyelet-trimmed one under her blue blazer, her stockings had blue ribbon threaded through the top, and her shoes were a shiny patent leather instead of the dull leather that was required. Her skirt had a thin sliver chain hanging from the side of it. He wondered how she didn't get in trouble for coming to school dressed like that.

The line moved another few paces, and Sasha could see the corner now, and around that corner and further ahead was the main office. This song and dance was required every year. You had to confirm your classes, and if you were able to swap out the ones you didn't want with new ones, space warranted. This process usually took the better part of the day, so actual classes didn't begin until Wednesday.

The girl in front of him looked nervous as the line moved forward. She toyed with the trim at the end of her shirt. He noticed then that her nails were painted, and now he really wanted to know whom she knew. He couldn't so much as get away with not wearing a tie. There was a low buzz, and the girl took out her cell phone from her pocket. Whatever was on the screen must have been something good because she seemed to bounce with her steps after she looked at it. The toying stopped then, and the line moved again. The group of six of them was at the front of the line. The four girls were called ahead, and Sasha and the girl rounded the corner, the tables now in full view.

She practically spun around and looked into his eyes. "What are you waiting for?" Her voice was like sparkles.

"To register." Sasha was confused.

"No, no, I mean . . . any wait list?" She shook her head.

"No," Sasha said flatly.

"Good." And with that, the girl turned around.

"What's your name?" Sasha didn't remember her from any of his classes, which was odd to him as he was senior.

"Muse," she said without turning around.

"Sasha," he said, completing the introduction.

Muse turned around then. "Sasha?"

"Yeah?"

Her disposition had changed. There was a wry smile playing on the corners of her face. "I've heard a lot about you," Muse said, the smile now blinding.

Sasha leaned over slightly and whispered back, "What?"

She said nothing for a few moments; she turned after and looked up into his eyes. There was a playfulness in them. "You'd really like to know, wouldn't you?" Muse whispered back.

He could live with that. He was mostly annoyed why he couldn't initially place her face with a name. It dawned on him then that she must be new, which wasn't out of the realm of possibility, but it was rare. What did she do to get kicked out of her previous school?

They were called to the room along with the other two people behind them, Faith and Oliva. They went to their respective tables, which were organized by last name. They both went to the first one.

"You're in luck, Drew. Archery is open. Want to register?" Ms. Colbert said as she scrolled on the tablet in front of her.

"Yes." Muse was beaming.

Ms. Colbert made a few clicks and then looked for her file that was close to the top. She edited one of the lines for classes with a pin and wrote down a number. "Just manually add this code to your bookshop list so you can shop for your materials," Ms. Colbert said as she handed over the folder.

"Yes, thank you."

Sasha watched as she left the room nearly bouncing.

Talented Friend

Amethyst

Now taking the identity of Gina, Amethyst let her hands burrow into the soft, dew-covered grass. Newburg Town wasn't any place special. Its crown jewel was a ski resort, but it was a major town bigger than Bluebird Stream, one that many runners wouldn't be taking because connections were hard to come by. All of it meant she could stretch her legs. She could walk among normal people doing everyday things like getting gas or shopping. Maybe they could stay an entire day.

Many of the plans were up in the air. Her mom was still waiting to get instructions from one of her connections. They were still headed to a unified territory, but which one was the question. Josh was getting food at the café across from the park she and her mom sat in. They just sat on the grass like it was any other day, and Amethyst couldn't remember the last time an activity like this felt so natural. Even during the last few months when they were still in the apartment, going places was a chore. She always made sure to carry every piece of ID she had that proved she was a Bluebird citizen. It was partly true. She was a citizen, adopted a second time after being put in an orphanage for Bluebird citizens, but legally and by birth, she was a Crow. Amethyst only knew the first part of the story, that she was adopted. She only knew how many times but not why.

Josh returned with sandwiches that had turned the opaque brown paper bag translucent on the way back. They ate them next to the man-made duck pond. In front of them was the pond, beyond that was a lush expanse of grass, and further still were five buildings lined up that looked like sailboats with their sails at full mast. They were this town's TerraTech campus. Amethyst tried not to think about their proximity. A short car ride through backroads was all that stood in the way between them and circumventing the Somber checkpoint. Her mom relaxed on the bench and looked up at the sky, watching the birds be pulled with light gusts of wind that danced across the surface of the water.

When they were done eating, her mom snapped back at attention, and they headed toward a safe house they'd been given directions to via a note handed to them by a guide. The guide also gave them car keys. It was the only instructions they'd gotten in the hours they had been waiting. The man was short and unassuming and was walking a small dog with an obvious left eye condition. He looked as if he was going golfing, but his physique made it obvious he had never been golfing or done any sport.

They would drive to the coast using the car across the street. Amethyst was ready to not be on her feet. She hoped no one noticed the damp and musky scent coming off her clothes and being trailed by her shoes. The car was a tiny box, and there wasn't any room to stretch out. Nonetheless, Amethyst liked that it was purple, and the seats were really leather. The smell of them masked her own scent. Josh drove and, for most of the ride, said nothing until the number of cars grew sparse.

"Is everything OK?" Amethyst could not help but ask. She was beginning to feel a little dizzy from the pain in her back, and she wanted to know if she would have to run soon or not.

"Everything is fine. We'll be fine. I just don't want to talk about sensitive information around anyone or anything that could be listening in. It's child's play to them." Josh turned another corner, sharing the road with a steady stream of cyclists, taking in the cherry blossoms.

It would soon be summer, and it was odd for Amethyst to think that this time last year, she was picking out first-year early college classes, and now she was out on the lam. Sasha decided to prolong going to college and instead took a couple of gap years.

It took only a few moments for all signs of other people to be spotty or altogether not there. The only houses were gigantic ones that appeared every few miles. And soon after that, the trees stretched farther and farther apart until all that was there was rocky coastline and wispy shrubbery. The safe house was just a few minutes away. Whoever it belonged to must have been very wealthy.

Josh slightly slowed as they curved around a bend in the road and slightly uphill, being once again enclosed by trees, but these were hundreds of years older and were almost comically huge. The house was smaller than the ones they saw spread in the woods but bigger than any place in Bluebird Stream.

Josh got a text just as they pulled into the driveway. It was a long list of names and nicknames: Juliana (Jules) Maykis, Robin (Robbie) Maykis, and Francy, who was labeled Dog. Pulling around the house, nearly in sync with their car as it was parked, was a Robin police cruiser, a deep bloodred with a bolt of yellow at the side. They locked eyes with the two officers inside, and Josh smiled.

"Come out. Smile," Josh softly said in Amethyst's direction.

Amethyst swallowed what she wanted to let out in the car, hurting her throat in the process. She smiled weakly and floated next to her mom. The officers got out and walked with a steady purpose.

"Good afternoon," Josh said.

It seemed to take them aback because they slowed their pace and nodded. "Mornin'."

The thick Robin accent was one Amethyst hadn't heard in person before. It was deep. The woman sounded almost like a man, but it also had a whistlelike tonal quality that was creepy.

"We got a call about a fire alarm going off. Is this your home?"

"No, no. We're visiting Jules. This is Gina, my niece, and her mother, Claudette."

"Ah, I see. Can we see some identification?"

"Sure." Josh handed over his license, and the officer took out her scanner like it was running away. It didn't beep, and she looked satisfied.

"Aren't you beautiful?" the woman officer said. It sounded like a question, and it was aimed at Amethyst. She quizzically looked over her features. "Can I see your identification?"

The other officer cleared his throat, and his face was washed in concern.

Amethyst gave her the papers and willed herself not to stand right next to her mom. Why would she be afraid? She was just visiting friends. The officer nodded and handed the passport back to her.

"We've seen a few runners passing through this area. I know it's controversial. I don't like to do it either, but if you see anything suspicious, call, and there's an automated form. You don't have to talk to anyone." She nodded as if she was agreeing with herself.

The officer left and drove down the pathway and toward another red-bricked house that looked utterly out of place in the middle of the woods. The safe house was a dark blue cabin with large front glass windows and a deep green door surrounded by a stone doorframe. All Amethyst could smell was pine, and it utterly covered her mossy, not-moss smell. "You don't think it's odd the police were just there?"

"No, that is not what I'm saying at all, dear. I find it surprising, but I'm sure it was all on purpose. Now that they think we personally know the family, they will leave us alone, at least for a few days. And if they watch us, we just act normally. I think I saw a small pool. It's only until we get further instruction." Josh spoke calmly. He thought it all genius to beat them to their suspicions and squash them.

Amethyst thought she would quickly source the biggest, fluffiest bed in the house and pretend for a long nap that she was at home.

Muse

Sasha

Sasha read the text again. He didn't know what to reply. In all honesty, he was still pissed off at Muse. He could just not reply to her and go about his life, find Zora on his own, and not tell her. She'd find out she was fine on her own. It made no difference. He liked Zora. It wasn't like he couldn't live without her but there was something there that made her the first thing he thought about in the morning.

Sasha opened his cell phone, slid past the home screen, and went through his text messages. Zora texted him for a period a couple of days ago, which was normal behavior for her. If she wanted to be left alone, she let herself fall off the face of the earth for days at a time. Muse was just suffocating, so she wouldn't know that. She probably texted Zora at odd hours and every day. Sasha only texted Zora when he needed her. It was the same relationship from the other end.

Muse texted him as he was going through Zora's social media, which was less updated than usual. She didn't even post photos of food as usual. Her mood status was set to happy; she had posted a picture a week ago of her white tennis shoes, a grassy field, and a long string of happy emojis. There was nothing to Sasha that seemed especially strange.

Zora was fine after the protest. She made it out and to the local supermarket. She didn't mention being tested when she came over a day after.

She didn't look afraid to him, but Sasha knew he wasn't good at gauging how afraid a person was. He tended to tune that emotion out in a lot of his interactions.

Muse's text was "Call me." Sasha called, and she picked up in one breath.

"Anything?"

"Anything what? I just got your message." Sasha sighed.

"But it's odd, right? Why would she take a picture of her shoes? She never takes pictures of clothes. All she cares about is food and dogs." Muse sounded like she wasn't taking in enough air.

"Where are you now, Muse?"

"Home."

"Is it OK if I come over?"

"No, you can't. Mom has guest over, and I don't want them in my business. I'll come to you. Give me a half hour or so," Muse whispered into the phone.

"OK, I'll see you, but I want to make it clear. I think Zora just wants to be left alone. But hey, if you miss me—"

"Like a bullet." Muse hung up.

The wind started to pick up outside and whistle through the air, twisting the curtains next to the open window. The air smelled like a mix of damp and smog. Sasha thought about how he'd work in an apology into the conversation when Muse got there. He wasn't sure how mad she still was at him. She wasn't ignoring him anymore, so that was a start, but the situation wasn't about their relationship but Muse and Zora's.

Sasha was scrolling through the message boards before the text, and he saw there was a demonstration at Ivy Ladder Mall. It was a ways from the square, but if he rented a van, he could take a few people and build more solid cases for his dad. You was already on her way to her birth parents after the corn husk doll demonstration. That was only one. It was like getting mice to take the bait. It eventually happened but usually only one. He couldn't get many at once. Most students were not like Muse or Zora. They didn't want to be involved.

When he met Zora, she was focusing on college. She wasn't aware she was a Lost Child. Either her parents lied at that point or she was one that was shuffled around to family after family. Sasha hoped she still didn't know. When the deal with his dad began, he was given a list of names and what schools they went to. His dad didn't make it that easy for him.

On Monday mornings, he would sit in the café of Talis University on the suburban side of Bluebird Stream and flirt with girls he saw. They would usually bite. Because of his dad's connections, he had a small following on social media. All he did was post about places he would hang out at around town. The more he kept it light and fun, the more people followed.

He met Zora before her economics class. She was working through a group of stats problems in a tiny purple notebook and drinking a *cortado*. Zora was lightly golden from the sun and had her black hair swept into a bun. She was polite and said "good morning" and nothing else. After a few Mondays, she sat next to him at one of the large tables in the center of the café. She said "hi" and just began to work on homework. The conversations were always short, of the "how are you?" and "I'm fine" variety.

When they had a full conversation, Zora looked like she was crying. She told Sasha she was failing the class without a "hi" and sat the textbook on the table before laying her head on top of it. Her long, feathery eyelashes clung together with tears. Sasha was uncomfortable. She didn't seem like the kind of girl to cry in public. The table began to fill with people, and they ignored the scene she was making. Sasha thought it must be common if it didn't faze anyone.

Sasha didn't bother finishing college after high school, so his Monday mornings was the most time he spent on a college campus in his entire life. Zora told him that she had only one shot to save her grade, and it involved a long group project with other people who were failing the class. She had no confidence that she'd get more than a C. Sasha didn't have any immediate solutions. He offered to do it for her, but she profusely shook her head. Sasha would've jumped at the chance if it were him.

Zora did end up failing the class, but she repeated it. Sasha signed up for the same class, so in the end, he did end up helping her by studying with her. Zora only had classes on the weekends these days, and weekdays were reserved for demonstrations in front of government buildings at nine in the morning. Sasha didn't know if she was doing better in classes now because they often didn't say much when they were in bed together.

Ivy Ladder was still floating around in his mind. Depending on how many people showed up, it could be grand. Ivy Ladder was a large glass cylinder building in the middle of a shrubbery maze. The demonstrators could fill the pathways from floor to ceiling and be hard to ignore. It was one of the more expensive malls, so the news was likely to come. They always cared more when a rich person's day was being ruined than a poor one. The visual of it was delectable. Things would be destroyed, and he knew that. TerraTech designed the mall and owned it. It could be a literal fortress if they wished it so.

Sasha didn't notice his phone vibrating in his hand as he fantasized. "I'm here" was written in all caps, followed by a smiley face emoji. It had to be sarcastic. She had also called twice. Sasha had returned from the coffee shop with minutes to spare before Muse came up, flurries dusting her shoulders, and started talking in waterfalls of sentences. "I went to her apartment, and there were so many dishes not done. I don't see her dog, but her dog's food bowl was filled with spoiled food. I think something is really wrong. We have to call her mom." Muse walked over to the window as she spoke and closed the window. "You aren't cold? It's like twenty degrees." Muse shivered. It was cute.

"You have a key to her house?"

"Key? No, I broke in." Muse laughed to herself.

Sasha had a key. He would've given it to her if she asked.

"I don't know where she could've gone. Does she have a boyfriend? Do you know if she has a boyfriend?" Muse looked him in the eye, serious, her hands on her hips. She hadn't even taken off her coat. She stood there in the living room, snow melting off her, with a big brown coat and huge tan hat that kept all her hair up. Her scarf was uneven, half of it trailing on the floor.

"Zora doesn't have a boyfriend, not that I know of. She just goes home. Sometimes she comes here and goes to class," Sasha said lowly; the worry was beginning to creep up on him.

"Zora never told me she comes here. Why don't I know these things?"

"Because she is a very private person."

"Wait, are you guys more than friends?"

"In a way, but that doesn't have anything to do with this."

"I don't like how you just sort of tell me things."

"It's not your business what I do during my downtime."

"Or who you do."

Sasha couldn't help smiling. "I have her mother's number. I'll call her. I'm sure she's OK. I think she would be on the news at this point if she was missing, the daughter of a TerraTech official."

Muse looked like she was short-circuiting when he said TerraTech.

"Yeah, her mom is in charge of District 5 storefronts. It's not research, more like programing but still . . ." Sasha smiled.

"How is she involved if her mom is one of them? Do you think she's in trouble?"

Sasha hadn't considered the possibility that her parents took the nuclear path and grounded her like she was a child. Ignoring it was what most parents were doing, ignoring the involvement unless the kid did something especially embarrassing. Zora tended to leave the scene before a large crowd began triggering the sirens and police started to flock toward them.

"There are more people in TerraTech than you realize. Many people are fed up. It's a job, not a political statement," Sasha said more to himself.

"How convenient for you. Is that even the truth?"

"Yes, do you want her mom's name?"

"Call her mom." Muse sounded like she was commanding him.

Sasha pulled up Ms. Jo'nest's number and pressed; it rang three times before she finally picked up. "Ms. Jo'nest, it's Sasha. I wanted to know If you've spoken with Zora lately?"

"Yes, yes. She came over a few days ago. We had a loss in the family."

"Oh, I'm so sorry."

"Do you want me to have her call you?"

"That's not needed. I just wanted to make sure she was OK, but I think Muse might want to speak to her." Sasha mouthed the words "loss in the family." So Muse could keep up with the conversation.

"I'll have her call her. Tell Muse I said hi. She always speaks so fondly of her. Such a sweet girl. I have to go, but I'll relay the message. Thank you for calling. Good night."

"I'm sorry." Muse pulled her scarf to the center.

"It's OK. Just trust me sometimes. I'm just related to my dad. I'm not him." Sasha held his arms out like he would encircle her.

Muse took a step back and shook her head. "I'm still really mad at you."

"Because you have a clear bias."

"This isn't on me. Zora isn't like you. She doesn't have a dad who controls nearly everything in the territory. He was on the news last night, talking about increasing security around the square. He literally lives in my neighborhood, but he wants to crack down on students living here."

"It's all just optics. He said the same thing last time, and nothing really changed."

"They started using dye—that was pretty big—and using that to test students."

"I won't let you be tested. I haven't let that happen." The lie seemed to settle in the pit of his stomach as he spoke. He knew that to close the case on her, she would need to be tested to confirm. It wasn't especially invasive, but it was embarrassing having it happen in public. He hadn't decided yet where he would let the case end. Their semiconnected group was growing. It used to be himself, Zora, Muse, Freddy, and Kira, but now there were three other groups of similar sizes all on the same group chat planning together. It was getting too big to keep up with, taking screenshots and forwarding to his dad. It was easier to just take a screen video of the walls of text. Each night a morning's paper worth of text was left. It felt so easy to relay information this way. It was almost becoming a reflex.

"I know that. I know. You just have some proving to do." Muse's voice was feathery. Muse left after that, and he could hear her boots squish with water toward the door. "Are you going to Ivy Ladder this weekend?"

"Most likely. Maybe we'll get a van."

"It must be nice."

"It's my own money."

Muse smiled and left. She always did this. She always did. With few words, she could make him feel entirely bare. She was very unlike Zora. Muse said everything that was on her mind and what she didn't like. Zora, on the other hand, was more inclined to let you figure it out and somehow feel guilty for not knowing. There were a lot of details about Ivy Ladder that he had to figure out like who he would have sent back and how much information his dad needed to know about it. He couldn't put them in too much danger. It might scare them away in the future.

Immediately, Sasha began texting his dad, "There's a protest at Ivy Ladder. I think I can bring Honest to them. WDYT?"

There was no response until later that night. "We already have her. Focus on Muse."

It was the last thing he wanted to hear.

Muse II

Sasha

The van cost a shinier penny than Sasha was expecting, but it was worth it in the end. He couldn't drive his SUV. There weren't enough seats, and it was tracked, and he didn't want to be stopped because of a failure of communication. He would drive the rented van to a parking lot down the road, and they would walk the rest of the way so they wouldn't arouse any suspicion. It was simply to get to point A to point B.

Earlier in the morning, his dad texted again, "Muse," with no other explanation. As if any was needed. It was like he was rudely ordering a sandwich and not a human girl.

The weather was nicer, and if it continued, maybe there'd be less puddles and potholes to dodge. Sasha shook his head as if to dislodge the thought of Muse being captured out of his mind. He didn't want to think about what would happen to her once she was in the custody of TerraTech. He heard stories of what happened to criminals, and technically, Muse was one, but she was also just stupid and young. She didn't kill anyone.

Zora didn't return any of Sasha's calls, but she did text back, "I'm fine," and nothing else for a full day. It was good enough for him. Any confirmation that she possessed physical well-being and cognitive function was enough for him.

If he did nudge Muse over to officers, how would he even do it without her being suspicious? Muse wasn't so dumb that she wouldn't notice she was being pushed into harm's way.

Freddy was simply a bonus. He fell when the corn husk dolls exploded into flames. It left him injured and unable to run. That was what his dad told him. Freddy knew he was a Lost Child, so usually, he was careful not to be caught and tested, but it was one fall that finally did it.

If it was an accident, maybe it could be easier, but there was a day at most left, and what could he possibly plan? Muse had made the situation perfect for Freddy to be caught. The fire and the ensuing commotion and running were the perfect formula. Sasha hoped he didn't have to start a literal fire to get her caught. He had no idea how large of a crowd would show, so there was no guarantee of reaching a decibel level high enough to trigger the sirens. That would definitely result in running. When the day came, all he could really do was just hope she did something stupid on her own. Muse was still Muse, and maybe that would be enough.

Muse hadn't really talked to him since Wednesday, and that bothered him. It was rare not knowing what was on her mind. She would literally paint a mural to show what was on her mind, but for the past few days, there was nothing, and the protest was the day after tomorrow. He saw her post on the boards as MadmamaYir, so he knew she would be there but nothing else. She didn't text him in the morning, she didn't send a random picture of what food she was eating or poorly made advertisements in the mall, and she didn't send him any stickers she found on the app store.

After he called the car rental company, he spent the better part of the day looking into the square. The Maykis statue was still covered in some soot at the base. The horse's hooves looked as though they were a pale green covered in black stockings. The glass from all the storefronts had been replaced that it looked as if nothing had happened. And there were two new cameras that he could see, but those could have very well been traffic cams because of their sheer size. His eyes somewhat burned from looking at his phone for so long.

Across the street in front of him, he could see a couple holding hands in front of the bookshop Inklings. It had been around for years, and he still hadn't been inside. The couple kissed, and the girl embraced him, swaying his body along with hers. He felt awkward looking at this and pulled out his phone. It was bare, but he knew, somewhere, his dad was at the headquarters, speaking Muse's name in his head like an incantation.

When the agreement between him and his dad began, it didn't seem like it would be too hard of a project. He just had to be a witness. They got in trouble on their own and he was only the final nail in the coffin. The reality of it was people were people and contrary to popular belief, people changed from day to day, minute to minute. He agreed to do it because people who were sent back seemed to get better. If they weren't quickly sent back, the medication that was developed by TerraTech seemed to help. He didn't want anyone to just be ripped away. That in itself was too traumatic but what good was happening with them just protesting and suffering in the middle of it all?

He ordered a sandwich from the grocery store beside his apartment complex and took a seat on the chair next to the window, staring at the overfull garbage can instead of the people below. His dad was expecting Muse, and he didn't know how to do it. She would need to be in the middle of something that either looked criminal or hurt enough that they would simply take her. He thought of this as he glanced around the apartment, taking inventory of the mess that was spilling out from the can, covering the kitchen island and the coffee table—so many takeout containers and newspapers. It usually didn't look like this, but he was helping Muse for many weekends with the dolls that cleaning got away from him.

After he had picked up his sandwich, he saw his dad had called. He couldn't pretend he did not see it, so after he finished his onion, turkey, and red pepper hero, he called him back. He picked up immediately. He sounded as if he was getting up from a seated position before he spoke. "Sasha, I hope you're doing well. I got your bills for this month. Is there anything else you need?"

"No, I'm OK, just busy." It had to have been the constant takeout. He usually didn't bring up his spending.

"I wanted to know what your plans were with her. Freddy and Kira weren't planned, and I hope you're working purposefully with her. She's causing more commotion. She triggered a few security alerts in the past week with her internet searches. I persuaded them to simply watch her, but I can't keep that up. It makes me look bad . . ."

"I know. She's very headstrong."

Sasha's dad grunted. That was not what he wanted to hear. It sounded too much like a compliment, especially for someone who could cost him his job. He cleared his throat. "How have you been feeling?"

Sasha hated this line of questioning. He felt OK, not great but OK. To anyone else, it was an innocent question; but at this moment, it just brought up the beginning of it all. It had been close to four years now, and he hadn't felt the effect of the gene anymore. It used to be a constant pain, but it was gone now, and to be reminded of it just brought up memories that were far too sharp. He remembered the date the pain stopped like it was his birthday: October 5, 2073. "OK," Sasha said firmly.

"I think you may need another dose. We've been noticing a resurgence of the illness. It is like it comes in waves, first in the teen years and again in the twenties. If this is a well-known issue, we may not need to test anyone, and now this is highly classified information."

"How often is that happening?"

"More often than I'm comfortable with. This started happening a few days after the protest, a lot of hospital admissions about hard-to-pinpoint illnesses. Most of those kids could be placed at the protest. I don't think it's some coincidence, but I can't figure out what triggered it."

"I don't know what to do about Muse. I don't think—"

"She's a security risk. She has to be dealt with. I'd rather not do it myself."

"She's not going to be committing any more arson. She was scared after."

"No, she'll do something worse. I can't share with you her searches, but she'll easily go to jail if she does them. That's if she doesn't die in the process."

"Oh, OK, I don't know how to do it." Sasha immediately registered the lost feeling in his tone.

"She just needs to be distracted long enough that we can surround her. Sasha, it's not that hard."

"If that's all I need to do."

"It is. Keep her from running with the rest of the crowd."

Sasha's dad hung up, and moments later, he got the notification that more money was deposited into his account. Sasha felt stuck in that moment. He wanted to help but how does one control the actions of a tornado.

Ivy Ladder

Sasha

They left a few miles from the city center in the van. Sasha had it delivered to a grocery store parking lot to not arouse any suspicion, not among the Authority but mostly among the other protesters. If Sasha triggered anything, his dad likely could explain it away for him. There was one other official who knew about the arrangement, and he was slightly up the ladder than his dad. Sasha knew this rendered him untouchable.

Muse sat next to Sasha with her hands tightly cupped on her knees as if she were steering the van with them. The day began soggy, but it was beginning to brighten up as they drove, the mist from the rain settling around them into puddles and creating rainbows. It wasn't a particularly long drive, but it certainly felt that way. All four rows were filled with mostly his former classmates. No one said anything, and Muse seemed bored. She was playing a connect-four game on her phone and humming a jingle from a car rental company, not the one they had used but another one, but all Sasha could think about was how annoying it was becoming.

About twenty minutes into the ride, the road became smoother, and signs for the mall became bigger and more ornate. It would only be a few minutes. The big rods of light were beginning to appear. At night, these would be stunning; but in the day, they were just large halogen rods sticking out of the grass at angles. The driver was Thomas, and he stopped next to a café as instructed so they could walk the rest of the way. Muse walked to Zora, and from the corner of his eyes, to Sasha, it looked as if she smiled. The mall was about an eight-minute walk away before they were at the entrance.

The parking lot was filled past capacity, and there were cars parked at the entrance that weren't real parking spaces, and some people didn't even bother parking but left the car at an angle at the entrance of the lot. They couldn't comment to one another about the size of the crowd when they entered because the crowd had drowned out all low frequencies with the loud boom of megaphones and shouting. It was a multitiered cake of people filling every level of the mall, shouting down to each lower level. The top level started a call and response, and each preceding level responded even louder than the last, enthralled with the competition. Moms covered their children's ears, and shoppers seemed to be leaving, ducking down as if the sound could not travel to the ground.

Sasha's band walked inside and stood around the fountain that was already four lines thick with people. Sasha looked over at Muse and noticed Zora was gone. Sasha walked up to her and smiled. She smiled sheepishly. "You see the ceiling?"

"Yeah."

"You won't see it tonight."

"Wait, what are you talking about?"

"Boom."

Sasha grabbed her arm and pulled her hard, attracting the attention of three people who looked like they were ready to break them apart. "When were you going to do that?"

"I'm not. Zora is. What is your problem?" Muse whispered hard.

"This is incredibly dangerous."

"I know this. But you know the only way they'll listen is if something big happens. Little bits of straw aren't enough to get people to pay attention!"

The sirens started, hurting his eardrums in the process. Muse crouched in pain, her mouth caught on a word and tears streaking her face. The running began sooner than she was expecting, and he was nearly knocked over. He grabbed Muse and started to pull her under one of the staircases.

"When the fuck is it going to happen, Muse?" Sasha was yelling, and he couldn't contain his anger.

"When the Authority shows up. Come, come." Muse began pulling him toward one of the stairwell doors between two shops. He moved sluggishly, stunned with the realization of what would happen. She produced a key as if by magic and opened the door. They were in a control room. The switches for the lights and gates and windows were all there.

"The black buttons are to trigger glass to break. You can do the honors if you like." Muse balanced a smile on her lips.

"No, no, we are not doing this. You cannot do this. I'm not gonna let you end up in jail for twenty years!" Sasha yelled, his spit landing on her cheeks and eyes.

"They are doing all this, and you're fine with it? It's OK for them to take students from classrooms and off the streets to test them and mark them as the enemy for no other reason but the fact that they weren't born here?" Muse took a deep breath, looking up at the ceiling. "I knew it. I fucking knew it! You're so incredibly fake!" Muse shouted even louder. She shook her head and walked backward into the door.

"I can't let you do this. You're already in danger. You saw that press conference. He basically called you a domestic terrorist. Said you had no regard for other people, and you're gonna prove him right. You won't win like this. You can beat him like this."

"I don't want to beat him. I want people to see what's really going on here, how hell-bent they are on just stealing us from everything we know."

"So you hurt a mall full of people?"

"They can run into the stores. They can leave."

"You've done enough protest to know it's not that easy. This mall is worth over a billion dollars. It's a fortress. Storefronts are going to explode if people start screaming. Muse . . . Muse? Are you listening to me?"

"You really thought that the buttons would be right here, all easily accessible like this? They are controlled remotely. You need a TerraTech phone or computer to trigger anything. I knew you wouldn't help, which is why I didn't ask you." Muse spoke in a forced calm.

"You really got Zora to help you with this?" As he spoke the words, the English sentence sounded so foreign to him.

"You're not being fair. People will get hurt," Sasha said more to himself than to Muse. He felt so sick to his stomach.

"We have another ten minutes. Zora will announce over the loudspeaker for people to get out of the lobby and into stores and then boom." Muse put her fingers tip to tip and quickly let them separate in the air, her facial expressions glazed over.

"Call Zora. You tell her you changed your mind. I'm not cleaning up your mess this time." Sasha's voice faltered.

"Stop talking to me like a child."

If he didn't do anything in that moment, it could all be lost. He would be disowned if he let Muse do what she was about to do. He could throw up. Muse was no longer looking him into his eyes.

If this were Zora, he could convince her, take her up into his arms, let the warmth of his breath fall on the nape of her neck before letting a kiss land there in the cavity between her neck and shoulder. He couldn't pretend. Zora was a tall brown-skinned beauty with long black hair and large brown eyes. Muse was a curly-haired, short, and puppy-eyed girl. She was a like a little sister he didn't want. Even thinking of what he was about to do felt incestuous.

As he walked over, she seemed to back away. He looked into her eyes as if they were the gate to her common sense and planted the kiss squarely on her lips; she didn't pull away, and he took it as the opportunity to deepen the kiss. Her hands were against his chest, stiff at first but then relaxed.

"I care about you. Please . . ." Sasha said onto her lips.

Muse said nothing, only tears streaking her face. "I can't call it off. It's too late."

"Goddamn it!" Sasha said through a clenched jaw. He pushed past her and ran down the hall. He would have to involve his father.

The siren began to blare in a new rhythm. He stood back against the shoe store and called his dad. Before his dad could say anything, he shouted, "Kill the electricity at the mall!"

"OK."

The lights still were as bright as ever. The sirens continued, and it began. One store on the first level burst. Screams were heard from outside as the glass flew across the linoleum. Four more stores in an unknown pattern exploded as the sound of shouting began, triggering whatever decibel was achieved. But then the water stopped running in the fountain, followed by a slow decrease of the siren. The power shut down, leaving only the center glass panel as the only gateway to light.

The call was still going when Sasha put the phone back to his ear. "It's done. It didn't happen. Thank you."

"Oh, you're thanking me. I haven't heard that in a while."

Sasha walked back and pushed himself into the room. "Come with me." He didn't have to convince her. She walked. He took her to an empty stairway. She said nothing as he began to text.

"You're really lucky." Sasha spoke each word like an individual sentence. There was nothing holding him together in that moment. His face and stomach were burning with anger. He could have called her stupid in that very moment, and he would be right, but that didn't seem sufficient to describe the gravity of what just happened. It was dark for a few moments before the lights began to turn on, first red for the emergency lights and then back to their bright white.

"I don't understand you. What is OK with you?"

"Obviously, everything that's wrong with you," Sasha said without thinking.

"Do you know what it would have done? They would have had to take weeks to reorganize. They wouldn't be able to mess with us. They'd be afraid. It would get even more attention—"

"This was enough attention. You're getting enough attention," Sasha said into his phone.

Zora didn't text back immediately, and when she did, it was only a random letter to indicate she had read it.

"We have to go before they show up. Come," Sasha said. He gently took her hand in his. She was still stunned, so he wouldn't have to be rough. She would simply follow.

"Zora is going to meet us at stairwell F." This was a lie.

"OK." Muse spoke toward the floor.

It was a long walk around the lobby to the back stairwell, and that was the point, to keep Muse out in the open and exposed for long enough for a member of the Authority to arrest them but really her. The ground was covered with glass and specks of blood.

When they were halfway there, the sirens began again, and a steady thudding began to ring from every set of stairs and the center escalator. It wasn't only the Authority but also TerraTech officials. They were a step above police officers because they were outfitted with far more sophisticated equipment. A few people yelled "run," and a stampede began and ended quickly when the shooting started. They weren't bullets but concentrated balls of sound frequency that stunned the victim. It left you temporarily deaf and blind.

Sasha led Muse to stairwell E and grabbed her by both arms before kissing her again. She was far more relaxed, and unlike the first time, she kissed back. This was it. This would be his only opportunity to finish this.

A split second later, Sasha could feel his hands being pried away from her shoulder and the gun in his back. "Hands behind your back!" a woman shouted.

They took all the protesters and zip-tied them into each of the stores on the first floor, the metal gates drawn into makeshift jail cells. A chant began. "Let us out! Let us out!"

And before Sasha could say anything else, he was shot. He found himself sometime later on the floor of a dressing room, being babysat by a TerraTech official away from everyone else. "You're up." The official spoke into her cell phone.

He had a splitting headache, and his vision was still blurry. "Where is she?"

"In the shoe store. A few more hours, and they'll all be processed, and you can go home."

He couldn't hear anything else that happened that night, but that didn't leave him without his imagination—Muse's small face looking up into the eyes of an official as her blood was drawn and she being told the known fact that she was a momentarily stateless person and then put inside of a van going down the road toward the local TT district office. The vision simply washed over him. He was too tired from everything to fight it.

❧

The national newspaper *Quill Inquirer* printed the story in ten full-color spreads on March 14. It was grainy, but it was still color. The Authority confiscated trucks of the paper that were headed to large college and high school campuses so it wouldn't cause disorderly behavior. Sasha's dad had one delivered to his apartment by the same woman who babysat him in the dressing room. He later found out her name was Regina Talis. Why such a big name was babysitting him was beyond comprehension.

His homework now was to name as many people he could see in the pictures. It would look bad if they arrested the wrong people. He was able to name ten; many of the other faces were distorted by the picture quality. Sasha's dad would use his statement to triple-check the cameras, arrest records, and citizenship documents. People often lied about who they really were, especially if it wasn't their first protest. Regina came back for the newspaper later in the afternoon and told him she was instructed to stay until his father arrived. She sat at the kitchen island.

Regina was taller than Sasha, and her hair looked to be a slightly darker shade of brown. Her eyes were a cerulean blue, and she was very pale. Cerulean blue was the Talis family trait. You didn't really need to say you were a Talis. People often knew with one look. The bed was on the opposite end of the room behind a cubed bookshelf. Here, Sasha sat and read over the article.

On March 14, an estimated seven hundred students caused mass panic and destruction at the Hunter's Point Mall in Ivy Ladder . . .

Five stores were triggered to explode from the amount of noise and chaos caused by the students . . .

TerraTech was called in to help make arrest.

Sasha's memory from yesterday was fuzzy. The stun gun they used made his thoughts feel foggy, and he wondered if it was a common occurrence. The only thing clear to him was that Muse was arrested right after the kiss. Her eyes were the biggest he'd ever seen them that he couldn't mistake the expression for anything else but fear. She also mumbled something as she was being dragged backward away from him, but he wasn't sure if that was true or if he simply imagined it.

Regina watched him the entire time from the moment she put the paper on the kitchen counter until he lay on his bed at the other end of the room. He was only slightly uncomfortable. This setup wasn't new to him. All his life, with the exception of the past year, he was watched by someone his dad had hired for the sole purpose of making sure he didn't do anything stupid or dangerous. They often didn't talk to him, play with him, or show any affection. Sasha simply regarded them as furniture.

"Your dad is on his way," she said in a thick Tol City accent. Her *a* sounds were fuller, and she just sped through the whole sentence.

Sasha wasn't sure what he wanted to talk about. Muse was already caught, and it would be back to the drawing board. He sat up on the bed, swung his legs over the edge, and let out a quick breath into his cupped hands as if he was blowing his nose. The thought of more work made him exhausted. Trapping Muse was emotionally draining. Kissing her felt very wrong, not so much for the betrayal but because he didn't have those kinds of feelings for her. Imagining her wondering if their relationship was romantic felt especially cruel to him.

It was about an hour before his dad arrived; he wore casual clothes instead of a suit, and water dripped from his shoulders as he pulled off his coat and tossed it over the coatrack. "Good work, Sasha." The words stung.

"Thanks," he called from behind the bookcase before walking over to the kitchen island, where they both stood.

"Over a hundred arrests were made, including Muse, and we're just waiting on one more." His dad appeared giddy as he spoke.

"Is she OK?" Sasha spoke carefully. She was dangerous, but she was also a friend.

"She's comfortable." He swiftly nodded before walking over to the kitchen counter and picking up the paper. "Ten." He spoke slowly, opening the folded paper.

Sasha disapproved, but maybe if he weren't shot, he'd remember more. "I'll let you know if I remember anything else, but those are the people I'm most certain of. I can help you build a case for them." Sasha walked closer, reaching for the paper.

"Who was involved in triggering the center pane of glass?" Sasha's dad looked him into his eyes. Sasha's own moss green eyes stared back at him.

"I'm not sure," Sasha said, speaking more to himself. What was he to trust about what Muse told him? It could have been all her. Zora may not have had nothing to do with it. Or maybe it was all Zora. He wasn't going to pin the entire thing or anything on either of them if he didn't know for sure.

"The phone used was of a TerraTech official. We won't know whose for a few hours. They've launched an investigation. In the meanwhile, I think it's appropriate that you're rewarded for your hard work. The little demon is captured and will be on her way home after some pesky paperwork, and you and I can finally have some piece of mind." Sasha's dad was animated, waving the paper around as he spoke.

"She's just a girl."

"Lover boy, she's not. She's been charged with conspiracy." He put emphasis on each word.

Regina stifled a laugh at the mention of "lover boy" and looked over at Sasha.

Sasha didn't want the kiss brought up, so he continued talking. "I think you should just send her back without anything extra. She's not this uncontrollable woman you're making her out to be. She cares about being kept with her adoptive family," Sasha stated matter-of-factly and was about to continue until he saw his dad's face blank, his eyes like emerald cabochons constricted inside an emotionalist stone.

"I think you're confused about what your role is. We already decided what the appropriate course of action is with your *friends.* We don't need your input beyond building a case. They are guilty. We're not going to do anything outside of what the law prescribes." His dad had sounded like he was reading from a textbook. Sasha knew that when he got like this, his mind was completely shut off from any common sense or shred of dignity. The conversation was as good as over.

"So do I get a reward?" Sasha realized it came out wrong as soon as he said it.

His dad sighed and then took out a thick wad of cash. It was partly in a small manila envelope, tearing the right side. "That's separate from your monthly allowance. I expect similar results in a month's time." He began to walk over to the coatrack.

"I don't have that kind of stamina." It was all a matter of reality, but it set off something because his dad began walking back.

"Without the distractions, maybe you'll find it easier." And with that, he left the apartment. Regina left shortly after, and with her eyes, she seemed to be apologizing for Sasha's dad.

March 3, 2071

Amethyst

The four chairs for the school heads of each class year sat empty on the stage. There wasn't any clarity to what the assembly was about, just a short one-sentence email without so much as a greeting. Sasha sat with one leg balanced over the other, and Muse was behind him. "I wonder who's in trouble," Muse whispered.

"It's gotta be bad. It's a testing day, but look, all my classes are blacked out." Sasha showed his class schedule; all the formerly green highlighted classes were know grayed out.

"A snowstorm is coming," Amethyst said, checking her own class list.

"Yeah, we will be expected to show up in our uniform for below-freezing days. They don't cancel classes. You know that," Sasha said.

He was right. Classes weren't canceled ever for snow. The dark blue snow pants she would be expected to wear were hanging in her closet.

"Dean Davis is coming now," Muse whispered.

Davis wore a petal pink suit, her steps perfectly measured as she made her way up to the podium. No one else joined her onstage. She looked over the sea of faces, with the track lights above, harsh on her skin, washing her out.

"In 2053, a famine tore through the Crow Territory"—she paused—"leaving many people starving or struggling to feed their families. The

Bluebird Territory and the Crow Territory came to an agreement to relocate the children suffering the famine to the Bluebird Territory. This agreement is set to expire next month. The children are now in high school." She paused. "This agreement will not be renewed, and those who were adopted, as a result of this agreement, will be sent back to the Crow Territory in stages, starting with the last names beginning with *A* to *I*." She didn't seem to finish before she left the stage.

A torturous cry erupted from somewhere on the left side in the front. Whispers erupted then. "What is she saying?" someone said, tears painting their speech.

Muse said nothing as she stood and left the auditorium.

Sasha was frozen. He looked down at his hands, which appeared to be trembling.

"They can't do that!" someone yelled from behind them. Daylight spread across the stage as the door to the outside world was opened. Dean Davis left. More people shuffled out of the doors, a lot of them in tears and a lot of them angry. Sasha still hadn't moved.

Amethyst felt the bile fighting its way up her throat then, and she couldn't help it. She threw up then, the yellow fluid seeping into the burgundy carpet. "You OK?" she could hear someone say. It sounded like Jaz.

She didn't look up. There was a napkin in her lap then. Sasha had stood up and was watching her. "Let's get out of here."

Muse looked as though her body was vibrating, her hands twisted up into a tight fist. Amethyst dug her hands into her pocket for warmth as she watched people walk down the steps. Two girls, sophomores, held each other, both crying.

Amethyst couldn't believe what happened. It all felt like a dream—a dream too vibrant to be reality. She knew about the famine. She was made to watch a documentary about it in middle school. It seemed like another time. The image of an emaciated child being carried around like a rag doll was burned into her memory. The wide-angle shots of empty farms and store shelves looped on the news every five years or so on the anniversary of when 80 percent of the crop failed. It seemed like all anyone had been doing since then was talking. The current president and the president before him met together with the Crow Territory president and comments were made about how important it was they working together. The reality of it was it was just constant talking and no action. The relocated children were always referred to as children, and it was as if they were trapped in time. Amethyst didn't really think about the children being her age and her classmates.

Amethyst didn't go back home immediately. She felt odd being out of classes early in the day. They waited for Sasha and walked to Pristine's. Sasha had to pick up his altered mask for graduation. He had been putting it off for a few days.

The shop sold books, Bluebird Territory masks, and coffee in the back. It was two stories with a spiral staircase in the center that led up to the seamstress who made the masks. They went up the staircase together and was greeted by Ms. Reeves. A long table had been set up with all the finished orders arranged by last name. The masks were kept inside dark blue satin boxes. The masks were simple, a thin strip with almond-shaped openings and a gold clasp that held ribbon ties.

"Yours is up here, Sasha." She tapped on the box next to the register.

"Thank you, Ms. Reeves." Sasha walked up to the register and took out a folded-up order form.

"Need a bag?"

"No, I'll just put it in here." Sasha put the box in his school bag and took out his card, swiping it.

"Can you believe how long it's been?"

"Hmm." Sasha nodded and turned back around to Amethyst and Muse.

Muse got a coffee, and they left the store, the ice-cold air hitting them in the face when the door was swung open. The bus stopped right in front of the store, which made getting back to the complex that Amethyst and Sasha lived in easier. Muse lived in the other direction, in the suburbs. They parted ways.

❧

It was a week later when the article was published. It was a two-full-page spread and printed in full color, each name color coded depending on class year. The names were in a much larger font than Rachel York's name that appeared on the left-hand corner. York wasn't in class that day, and the rest of the newspaper club was in school for a time before they were yelled out of the school café when people began to find the article.

Muse laid out the paper in front of Amethyst and Sasha, her body seeming to sway above it. She pointed to her own name, *Muse Ophelia Drew*, nearly at the top of the page. Slightly above was *Sasha Cayden Ashford*. Her eyes were wet. Amethyst wanted too badly for Sasha to say something, but he didn't.

Amethyst looked away as she noticed Muse's finger sliding to the opposite page, potentially looking for her name. She didn't want to look. She didn't want to know.

"Millen," she said quietly. She didn't need to finish the thought. Amethyst had never told Muse her last name. She was the only person in the school named Amethyst and the only Millen.

"Please just throw it out." Amethyst spoke into the air.

"Why are you trying to ignore this?" Muse's voice was dripping with disgust.

"They are still in the middle of negotiations. Nothing could come of it. We could be left alone. You don't know what they're going to do," Amethyst said softly.

"Yeah, we don't know," Muse spat back.

"Hey!" Sasha stood.

"What? What? Did you know they already started to send back people? Four from Talis Technical," Muse said.

Amethyst shook her head as if it would dislodge the thought from her head. There was a lot of names. Most of them were juniors like her.

"Yeah, and they want to make us next," Muse continued.

"She probably didn't know. You're being cruel." Sasha raised his voice.

"You knew?" The words were barely audible.

"I always knew." Sasha was looking directly into her eyes.

"A few years . . ." Muse was calmer now.

There were a few moments of silence before Muse broke it when she moved the chair from under the table and sat down. Sasha sat back down and closed the paper, which Amethyst was still staring at.

❧

The news was on in the living room when she came home from school. Her mom, sat with a large fuzzy white blanket across her lap. In crystal clear clarity was Luke Talis standing at a podium, his one green and one blue eye unsettling her. He had just finished his speech, with the crawler saying that negotiations were underway as Muse had said. Something faltered inside her, and she couldn't so much as take off her coat, let alone put down her backpack, but the tears flowed then. Her mom got up from the couch and embraced Amethyst. She landed a few kisses on her cheeks before she could pull away.

"I'm sorry," her mom said before Amethyst could take enough air in her lungs to produce a word.

It wasn't enough. It wasn't nearly enough, and she could feel a new emotion welling up inside her. It was heavy. It made her mind feel sluggish. Amethyst didn't know what to say. She had always suspected, but she dismissed her thoughts for the protection of her own heart. Now it was different. She didn't know anything else. She had been a Bluebird for as long as she could remember. The Crow Territory might as well be a foreign country.

Her mom rubbed her arm, melting the flurries that were left on contact. "Come. Let's get you out of these cold clothes," her mom said as she removed her backpack.

"When were you going to tell me, or were you never going to tell me?"

"We'll talk about this later, when your dad gets home."

"No." Amethyst's voice came out strained like the words had fought their way up her throat. "York wrote an article that has all the names. My name was there and Sasha and Muse and basically everyone in my class. When were you going to tell me?"

"We were going to tell you. We didn't expect this—"

"Expect that the deal would expire? You expected to just keep me for yourself." The words felt wrong in her mouth. She hadn't entirely felt that way, but she would've liked to know. She didn't want to leave.

Bells

Amethyst: June 9, 2071

It was the fourth class of the day and Amethyst's emptiest. Sasha was switched in to help fill it out so pairs would be possible. The teacher still hadn't arrived. Amethyst sat at the front, looking at the notes on the board from the previous class, trying to piece together what they were talking about. When the teacher arrived, there was a symphony of pushing in of chairs and shuffling of paper. The atmosphere of the class had changed in the last few weeks.

Graduation was in a few weeks, and the seniors either didn't come unless there was a test or showed up out of uniform. The teachers noticed, but they couldn't do much since it was most of the class. The main office had a limit. The prefects didn't bother to do anything, and half of them wore their white blazers over jeans. The dean was nowhere to be found most of the time. Muse told Amethyst in passing that she thought she was fired or went on leave. The story was unclear.

Hobbs began writing on the board; he wrote in gentle, sloping letters, "Fictional dream."

A paper ball flew across the room, and a peel of laugher erupted from the back. Hobbs said nothing. He took off his messenger back and sat at his desk, his face clear of any emotion. "Spend the next couple of minutes talking with your partner about this concept," Hobbs said to his folded hands. He sighed.

No one said anything at first, but then conversation erupted. No one was talking about fictional dream or any kind of dream. Sasha sat next to Jaz, who was twisting her blond, nearly white hair around her hand. Jaz said something low that Amethyst couldn't hear, and then she gathered her things, stood, and left the class.

"Mercer!" Hobbs called out to her. She didn't so much as look back.

Amir was the prefect in class and was sleeping. Under normal circumstances, he would have given her a demerit.

"There's still nearly a month left of class." Hobbs got up from his chair and started walking toward Amir's desk. He was lightly snoring, his spiral-bound book under his arm. Hobbs put a hand on his back. Amir didn't so much as budge. "You have to finish somewhere. Better if you do it now than next year."

"I'll leave with a B. I could live with that," Sasha said.

Hobbs looked at Sasha then, his brown eyes hard.

"What's the point if we're gonna have to start over in the Crow Territory anyway?" Amethyst said as Hobbs made his way back to the front of the room.

"Excuse me?" Hobbs looked confused.

"Half of us will have to start our last year over again," Sasha clarified.

"So you don't bother. You think Crows think this way?"

"How would we know?" Amethyst found anger creeping into her tone.

"That subject is off limits for the time being," Hobbs said, walking over to the door and propping it open.

"Why?" Amethyst stood, her body leaning slightly forward as if she wouldn't be able to hear the answer otherwise.

"It simply is. It's too sensitive for the moment," Hobbs continued.

"For you?"

"Take a seat, Millen."

Amethyst didn't know what took over her body, but she found herself walking to the front of the class. Sasha shifted in his seat.

"If you would like speak with the guidance counselor—"

"Why can't we talk about it?" Amethyst took a few steps closer.

"This is not the place," Hobbs said flatly. He looked nervous.

Amethyst felt a mixture of nervousness and anger settling at the pit of her stomach. Hobbs texted someone then, and Amethyst walked backward into her seat.

"Take a seat," Hobbs repeated, the tone threatening.

Two prefects arrived shortly after. "Amethyst Millen," the curly-haired one said.

❧

The day ended without further incident, and Sasha walked Amethyst to the bus. He was going the opposite direction to meet up with his dad.

"I was about to pull you away from him. I'd never seen you so angry." Sasha took off his sweater, a stiff wind circling them.

"I'm fine. I don't want to talk about it."

"There's going to be a protest in front of the school next Wednesday. Walk out and join us."

"My mom would kill me. She's probably already saw I got a demerit today. I'll have to explain that somehow."

"Your mom will understand." Sasha sounded really sure.

"I don't want to. I just want to be in bed. It's hot."

"OK." Sasha threw his arm over Amethyst, and he walked her the final block to the bus before planting a kiss on her forehead and leaving toward Persimmon Street.

Dreaming of Arestromer

Amethyst

The down comforter was so heavy that Amethyst could feel the weight of it pressing lightly on her legs and stomach. Josh had taken her mom to the pool around back, and she could hear the sounds of chatter from down below. The house was like a castle. Every window on the first floor was floor to ceiling, and everything outside was so green and appeared to be magnified by the glass.

Amethyst was unable to sleep despite more than an hour of trying. She kept replaying the scene of the police officers in her mind. They seemed a little by the book, if that made sense. It was like they were reading from a script. Nonetheless, she knew this was all temporary. They couldn't stay for longer than a night or two before heading toward Somber. It was just a short drive through the woods, and the thought excited her more than it worried her. They were only days away from Arestromer. She could almost picture herself on an actual beach, looking at the ocean ripple and pull away from the coast and feel the grit in her shoes and uncovered sun on her back. A few days were all that stood between her and a beach getaway. In this fantasy the pain was gone. She had reached Dr. Miles and his cure had worked.

Arestromer was also freer in other ways. They didn't have the Authority like the other territories. The Authority was like police officers, but they only controlled the aspects of life that were social. They didn't allow people under twenty-five to participate in disruptive and otherwise "rancorous" activity. This was a new law. This was the law that gave them most of their power because it meant they could stop protest. Most of them were quiet and peaceful, but their argument was it disrupted the school day and business hours having that many people blocking the streets on a business day.

Amethyst regretted never being deemed disruptive. She did very little to stop anything. All she was doing was running, and this thought had stayed front and center in her mind before the act from the moment her mom began to talk about leaving the unified territories.

It was hard to not think of the Authority patrolling the streets. It was hard to not know exactly what they looked like or what their voices sounded like because they often were classmates. The Authority wore dark blue uniforms with an embroidered heron on the back to differentiate from the bluebird on police officers' uniforms. The heron's head and neck wrapped around from the back to the back of right sleeve and finally to the front. They didn't understand the difference. They still acted as though they were police officers and arrested people on minor things.

Amethyst remembered when she was nearly arrested when she asked for clarification from her teacher about why the Lost Children were being sent back. She felt that she could have stopped there, but it just made her so angry that she asked again why it made sense. It came to a point where she stood from her desk and was halfway to the teacher's desk. She knew Mr. Hobbs didn't have the answer, but she wanted another answer other than the one that it was going to be the law. It wasn't a real answer, and Amethyst knew this. The law was murky, hence the creation of the Authority. They were the ones who pacified the Crow Territory officials when they deported the Lost Children back for breaking laws. If you were deemed an enemy of the state, you lost your citizenship.

Amethyst got out of bed and got dressed. She considered just staying dressed until they left. She already had showered. In her jacket pocket, she hid her cell phone she had previously charged on the off chance Sasha would finally text again.

She was a wooden chair at the window that overlooked half of the trees in the castle-like mansion. She took out the phone and looked at the lock screen for a moment before swiping. The message board was highlighted in yellow indicating she had a message. It was spam. She scrolled the board, and it wasn't anything she hadn't seen before. The near explosion in Ivy Ladder was the most talked about. The words that were the most used were bolded so anyone could click to them and see the related post. Domestic, Terrorist and, Muse were the most used words. There was a link to a press conference. Sasha stood right next to his dad and something about this visual made her heart sink.

Perhaps it was because he was there, and she was here. Everyone was scattered in the wind. Perhaps it was because he looked trapped there. Amethyst couldn't imagine what it must be like to have your dad be wrapped up in those people. But that still wasn't it.

Something was off about her feed and on closer inspection she noticed the thread for Dr. Miles was locked and Amethyst couldn't access it. This only happened when a thread was archived. She couldn't even read any of the words from the thread's description because it had been blurred. The admin of the thread was covering their tracks.

Press

Sasha

Sasha took the words he said, and they seemed to only find his way to his mouth that twisted up into a snarl. His mind was blank. The driver careened the car up to the sidewalk to let him off.

His dad, who didn't turn around once to talk to him directly, said flatly, "I love you. Don't get into any trouble." In his hand was a hefty envelope of cash about three inches or what one would call a bribe in English. Beside him, Hakeem was holding him by the shoulder, pushing Sasha into the seat to prevent him from lunging toward his father.

"That's all you're going to tell me? Away? Away to where?"

"She's a criminal. Don't worry about her."

"She didn't get a trial. There was nothing. What the hell is this?"

"She had one. She was found guilty, and she was dealt with."

"Please just tell me she's alive." Sasha let out a ragged breath, with his head in a bow and the rest of his body twisted up, unable to uncoil. The stack of money too large for his hand to comfortably hold began digging into the middle of his right thumb and pointer finger. Sasha's dad whispered something.

Instead of unlocking the door, the driver parked the car. Sasha hadn't noticed the way they were headed until the car came to a complete stop. Flanked at both sides were large light rods punctuating the road. Floating slightly above a small grouping of hills was the roof to the Bluebird Terra-Tech headquarters. It gleamed like a diamond in an evergreen ring setting. Every other pane of glass was covered with lush greenery. The others were a smoky black to obscure everything happening inside.

"You're going to come inside and watch me give a speech about the protest. You are to keep quiet, unless one of my colleagues greets you. Keep interactions short and impersonal. Understood?" Sasha's dad turned his attention to his phone, waiting for his boss to send the pass code so he could make his way inside the compound. Access was granted daily and in some cases hourly. The only persons who had unfettered access were the head of the corporation and relevant government officials. The Maykis, Snow, and Talis families were the only exceptions to this rule, but they rarely exercised that power.

When the process of sending the children home started, the access of Sasha's dad became more restricted to only the labs he was working in. He had to wait like a courier to get into the front door. He was due to give the speech in the First Hall which was directly through the lobby. Lining the curved wall enclosing the compound was news vans. It shouldn't take long to give the apology for his reckless behavior and pass it off as teenage angst. The sooner his dad could give this speech, the sooner he could go back to actual research.

"I'd rather stay in the car," Sasha said as he watched newscasters pounce onto the pavement, some being ushered in by small groups of security guards. "I can't be seen with you. What will Muse think? It would completely ruin my credibility." Sasha became more aware with each word.

"Your credibility is already shit as is mine. The least you could do you for me and you is to clean up this mess before you start applying to colleges so you can at least go somewhere. I'm fine with you going to one of the unincorporated territories. Just go somewhere instead of chasing girls," he said as he looked onward toward the long line of personnel.

A crisp "phulk" vibrated from his phone, the code flashed, and his dad showed it to the driver. There was no time for Sasha to avoid being seen once the code was punched in, and they moved only feet from the keypad. The car was surrounded by flashing lights and questions that drowned out one another.

This wasn't a new experience to Sasha. Every other time, he could simply drown out the noise; but in those instances, he didn't care about being seen. He wasn't the center of attention. His father was. But now he was just as on display. Sasha let the envelope fall to the ground and lowered his head. He could avoid some flashes. He could try to look less like he wanted to be there. On one hand, he wanted to take this opportunity to find a substantial heavy object and toss it in his dad's direction; but on the other, he imagined all the scenarios in which Muse would cry once she saw this news spread. He still didn't know what exactly happened to Zora and now this. It was a trap. He was trapped. He also wasn't dressed for a press conference so how much would they believe of it while he's dressed like they pulled him off the streets. He guessed a lot. A "problem" child wouldn't dress properly for appearances.

The First Hall was a room he'd been in at least four other times. Most of them were before tension with the Crow government wasn't so strong. Sasha remembered his dad saying there wasn't going to be a war. And he was right. There wasn't a war. There were just his classmates being arrested by police and thrown onto the pavement.

The driver stopped just in between the gate and left the car. He stood next to Sasha's door, poised to open it. Sasha steeled himself, picked up the money, and put it in his jacket pocket. He looked like a kid they picked up from the street. His jacket was a tasteful navy blue blazer, but he was wearing a graphic T-shirt that read, "Fuck it." At least it was in the font closest to cursive, that being italics. The cuffs of his jeans were frayed from rubbing against the pavement. He missed how long his pants would last when they were properly tailored. All he had to do was act like he belonged, which was becoming harder and harder.

The door was slid open, and a wave of light pierced his eyes. They kept only a foot of distance between himself and their equipment. A small brown-haired woman just gawked as she took pictures. She must have been an intern. The conference room was large but not large enough for the van after van and car after car that arrived. Some people had their backs against the wall, and at a certain point, they didn't run out of chairs but space to wheel in stacks of chairs. It could not have been legal.

Sasha stood right next to Hakeem; unbeknownst to anyone watching, he wasn't his bodyguard but only his dad's. Sasha's bodyguard was more of a keeper, and he quit nearly four months ago. Sasha liked to give him the runaround.

Techs were running around, doing last-minute sound checks, and more security in red uniforms took their stations at every exit. He took a sip of water.

"Thank you, all, for taking the time to attend the conference. I know it's a tough decision to choose this over the Citizen's Day ceremony. This will be about not only the actions of my son, Cayden Sasha Ashford, but also the trials we have begun to treat the illness common in relocated children from the Crow Territory."

Relocated? Sasha internally groaned.

"The actions that took place on the thirteenth of March were reckless and dangerous and show not only the kind of negative influence so-called citizens like Muse Ophelia Drew have on the general public but also how little they care about the danger it poses to bystanders." Marcus paused, resting his gaze on the young reporter he saw visibly angry at his words. She reined in her expression.

"These children are mistaken about our intentions at TerraTech. They have convinced themselves in their echo chambers that we seek to hurt them, that we derive some pleasure from breaking families apart. We only know that, through our research, these children, now young adults, who go home recover from this mysterious illness at a faster rate and are less likely to die." Marcus took a sip of water.

Sasha asked himself, *But why? Why do they recover?* It was a question that had not been answered by anyone and it was driving him mad.

"By microdosing with the drug still in the trial phase, we have discovered it slows down the progression by two months, which can ease the transition of these teens as they are processed to be returned home." Marcus put his right hand up before any reporter could ask a question.

"I'll take any questions in writing by using the kiosk in the lobby. In the next room are refreshments. I'll choose which questions to answer in an hour."

He pinned it all on Muse, every bit of it. Just like that, his dad just cleaned up the last year. Muse really wouldn't speak to him now, and that was exactly the point of all this, even if he tried to be upfront as possible, tell her everything, tell her about his dad's drug, tell her that he and Zora were in a relationship—but no. She'd believe him, but she most likely wouldn't talk to him in the first place. His dad was only a few letters away from calling her a domestic terrorist. How would he even get in contact with her. She was most likely in the Crow Territory by now. There would be no way his dad would give him the information to contact her.

"Come, I have something to show you." Marcus nodded to Hakeem, who then pulled Sasha along by his arm like a five-year-old. They went through a few high-security corridors until they were in the lab his dad worked in. It was empty, which was odd for a Wednesday morning.

"I'm impressed at your restraint. It only took you twenty years to learn the meaning of no." Sasha's dad walked over to his office, which was in the center, surrounded by a dome reinforced with glass and steel.

Hakeem pushed Sasha forward. As he walked even closer, Sasha smelled a scent potent and familiar. It smelled sweet, like melted sugar but woody like basil and bark that had been boiled for a long time to the point it can make your eyes water after a certain period. Lying in a metal tray was a prepped syringe.

"I want you to be one of the first. If my calculations are correct, the last dose I gave you will wear off in a week or two. I'll give you another two. A month to do what I ask of you." Marcus began washing his hands in the sink behind his desk.

"What more do you want with me?" Sasha pushed the metal chair in front of his desk, knocking it over.

"I want Muse to go home with her birth parents." He dried his hands and put on a pair of lilac gloves. What he really was saying was he wanted Sasha to give a statement of what she was going to do so she would be deported out of the country.

"Yeah, fuck you." Sasha began walking away, but Hakeem grabbed him and, with little effort, tossed him onto his ass. He was blindsided before he could react to the syringe being inserted into his shoulder. It took a split second for the drowsiness to kick in.

❧

Sasha opened his eyes; the hazy, mind-numbing feeling was now localized to his forehead and no longer his entire head. His room had been abrasively cleaned. The sharp sting of aerosols dug into his nose as he took a deep breath. He stopped moving when he realized the cuffs on his left wrist holding him to the birchwood post of his bed. They were a gunmetal silver, so shiny that they looked faux.

His phone was right beside him, facedown. He hoped there was still some charge left. There was some charge, 65 percent, enough for a few phone calls. Put as a screensaver, there was the message "You are under temporary house arrest."

Sasha pulled at the handcuffs to test his range of motion. It was limited to the point he could lift his body from head to waist, but he couldn't lift his body more than about a sixty-degree angle. He did the only thing he could think to do, and that was patrol the boards for anything new.

He checked Netixy, and it was bone dry. So was Convi. He closed the app and refreshed to see if that was it, but there was nothing. Both apps showed you what was popular in your area, and that was it. If it didn't gain any likes, it simply vanished and only appeared if you searched for that particular topic. It was odd that he couldn't read any post, not even ones about the weather, which were always there. People loved to wholesale gripe about the weather.

He looked at his settings to make sure he didn't turn slumber mode on. It turned off all functionality for apps. It was the only way he usually got homework done. His settings were frosted over from use. He couldn't change anything. The only thing his phone was capable of was calling, texting, and using the map feature.

The only person who could disable his phone was his dad, and he didn't doubt that his dad had done it, but he couldn't think of why. He was still on a mission to destroy Zora's life, so he needed more than the basic features of his phone. He hoped, at first, this meant he didn't have any more to do with the mission and that all his responsibilities were gone. He could just live in an apartment on his own and do whatever he wanted without any strings and didn't have to think about how he would destroy the lives of people he just met. But that would be too easy. His dad would've said something. He always loved to talk.

Regina showed up, opening his door with a key she got from Sasha's dad, and said nothing as she opened the handcuffs. "I'll unlock your phone for you," Regina said like she was talking about a casual subject like the weather and held out her hand. Sasha handed it to her and watched as she turned it off and on and then quickly did a few swipes on a dark screen before a black pass code screen appeared, waiting for input. She punched in a code and then handed him over the phone.

"Why all this?" he said, looking at the revived phone in his hands.

"You should be able to figure it out." Regina nodded before turning away to walk toward the door.

"Wait, just tell me. I don't have the mental energy to deal with any puzzles right now," Sasha called after her.

"Zora's been arrested. They discovered her hair in the mall's control room," Regina said without even turning around.

What am I supposed to do at this point? was the thought that sank in his head like a lead ball. Muse and now Zora were in permanent custody. A quarter of the group was now gone, and Sasha realized they were all from his faction. A thought that began to come front and center was that Muse really did plan to explode the large center pane of glass in the mall with Zora's help. Zora would probably get life in prison for using a TerraTech official's phone for illegal activity. Eventually, Muse would be connected to the crime, if she wasn't already, and he'd never see her again except on television or on newspapers.

He felt so separated from them now. Nothing he did would change the situation they were in, and his dad didn't really need him to get Muse back with her parents now. Zora was smart enough to sell Muse to the Authority and TerraTech to save herself.

Strangely, he felt a little lighter. The nightmare was now realized, and nothing could possibility be worse than they were now. Zora and Muse were the only two members of the group whom he was close to. Anyone else he added to his count would simply be faceless. He was forgetting what Kira looked like, and he didn't even know her last name without looking at his documents. He only knew it began with an *A*.

Citizen's Day

Amethyst: August 8, 2071

The windows to the student center were filled with all the faces of the ones who had fallen, their names, and their schools. Each pane contained at least two dozen pictures of students in their uniforms. Amethyst recognized a few of them. Cluttered against the wall were candles, many of them half burned; dirtied stuffed animals; and wilting flowers. Written in spray paint was "Lost Children" in all capital letters. The pictures filled her with a heavy feeling that she couldn't describe. All the major news outlets were talking about how the Falling only happened to relocated Crow children. There was no other rhyme or reason. It all seemed very random besides that one joining detail.

Amethyst's mom and dad didn't say anything as she stood next to the outside of the scaffolding. The bus was still about ten minutes away, running every twenty minutes. They would ride it into the square, which was twenty minutes away, the last stop the bus would take today on account of Citizen's Day, always designated on the president's birthday. Most of the booths that were set up on this side of town had petitions to keep the children who were adopted in the territory.

Her mom and dad were holding hands as the bus arrived. Amethyst ducked under the scaffolding and joined them.

The bus was filled with people. Most of the girls had their hair done in blue ribbons and thread, their faces covered in lattice designs partially obscured by their mask. The men had painted their upper arms in simple stripes to an intricate tangling of thorns. They held on to the polls near the door, and the bus pulled off.

Amethyst couldn't shake the sinking feeling inside. It always caught her in the middle of a thought and dragged her down. She hadn't bothered to get ready that morning. What would really be the point? She wasn't like the happy people who surrounded her. She wasn't like her mom or her dad. She wasn't born in the territory. She wasn't meant to be there. She shook her head, and the woman sitting across from her stared. She must have looked foolish shaking her head in response to nothing.

Checkpoint

Amethyst

Amethyst and her mom with Josh left the castlelike estate sometime before dawn. When they climbed inside the SUV, the sun was cresting around the mountains in the distance. It would be the last of the sun they would see until much later as they wove through the thick woods. Every mile or so, the car would get stuck in thick mud, or there would be a broken-off tree branch on the path. The road smoothed out as they were approaching the highway that would bring them to Somber.

"Charlotte?" Arnett said in a serious tone.

Amethyst had learned to smile and nod at whatever name her mom called her. Her new name was now Charlotte Ren Fairweather. It was a lot as a name, but she only had to remember the first part. The Burly Loop to Somber was the most backed-up highway they had been on since the beginning of their trip. The checkpoints were gone according to her mom's contacts, but they were driving at eight in the morning as everyone else was commuting to work.

"You have your paperwork ready?" Josh said as he changed lanes to drive toward Arestromer.

Arnett nodded and took out the thick stack of travel papers. The paper was powder blue, bound in brown leather.

As the day wore on, the sun hung higher, beating down on the car and in their faces. Amethyst was beginning to get flushed and irritated. In one fluid motion, she unbuckled her seat belt and lay down across the third row to avoid the gaze of the sun. It was cooler, but the seats were still warm, almost unbearably hot, especially the metal slots were the belts were fed into.

"Another twenty miles. It will be over in no time," Josh said from the driver's seat, chewing on gum as he glided for a short distance behind another SUV, this one with Talis University stickers and plates.

"My cheeks are so hot," Amethyst said, feeling the heat beneath her skin and the small bumps.

"Did you eat something strange at the house? It looks like an allergic reaction." Arnett turned to get a better look and handed Amethyst her mirror.

"Does it burn at all?" Josh asked.

It stung when she touched it, but she wasn't sure if that was the same thing. "No, but it stings. I don't wanna touch it." Amethyst fanned her face. It had to be the heat. It was the only extreme in her environment right now. It had appeared so fast. Just moments ago, she was touching her cheek to wipe away the crumbs from breakfast. All she had was eggs and some bacon between a biscuit. The heat had never bothered her. But just a few hours in eighty-degree weather was causing specks to appear on her face.

"Maybe we can stop, get something for the rash. It looks like it's around your eyes," Josh said as he looked at the exit signs.

Amethyst hadn't opened the mirror yet, but she did then, pulling it from the middle compartment between the seats where her mom had stored her makeup after finishing it this morning. It was everywhere. Her face was raw and splattered with darker red specks. It was on her cheeks, her nose, and around her eyes, almost like a mask. The only place it had not touched was her chin, but she was convinced if she looked long enough, it would appear there too like magic.

"Oh, I'm so sorry. How does your throat feel?" Josh asked as he put in "drugstore" on the GPS. It was much nicer than theirs; it talked back and showed three-dimensional renderings of the neighborhoods, complete with people and periodic animals like dogs and pigeons. The nearest drugstore was closer to Somber. "I don't think we should continue to travel while she's having a reaction to something. I think we should take her to a doctor, make sure it's nothing serious."

"Maybe it's something related to the illness. I don't want anyone pinpointing her as one of those children. I think we should wait until we're in Arestromer. She doesn't have any breathing trouble, right?" The way she said "one of those children" was saturated in disgust. It bothered Amethyst.

"Right," Amethyst said, her gaze unbroken from the mirror. It was so ugly. It looked like a combination of sunburn and acne. The only difference was that the redness was with light brown undertones that it looked like rust.

"Is that what you want, Amethyst?" Josh turned slightly.

"Yes, I want to keep driving," she said as she closed the mirror.

As the sun began to set, the burning sensation began to go away, but what didn't go away was the sensation that there was something on her face. Josh stopped for food about fifteen miles in and went solo to a diner. Amethyst ate slowly; the rash on her face made the movements of her mouth hurt. *I can do this*, she told herself. It would only be a little while longer, and maybe then she would have some medicated cream in her hand and be under an actual blanket and not sleeping with her head bent to the side of a seat belt.

There weren't many words passed between Arnett and Josh after they passed by the drugstore. He tried to convince her a second time, and she simply didn't respond. Amethyst sided with her mother. The more stops, the riskier it became. She didn't want to find herself arrested for running all over a face rash. It was painful, but she wasn't dying. She had already experienced enough pain from whatever mysterious illness to know that she wasn't going anywhere because of it. She was strong enough to get through it; what would another few days really be in the grand scheme of things?

The famous gray-blue tint of Somber began to shift the quality of the sky. The air smelled saltier but at the same time floral. It didn't take long to see them—tall rods stuck in the ground like Zeus's bolts of thunder. A large sign was held up by one of the officers, commanding each vehicle to yield. And at each one was a pair of Maykis Isle police cruisers. They stood in reflective vest with large-brimmed hats and tall brown boots. Three white horses stood at the edge of the highway, stirrups pulled up by their riders. Amethyst was glad it was dark. She didn't have to show anyone her blazing red face.

Charlotte . . . Charlotte . . . Charlotte. The more times she repeated the name in her head, the more it sounded alien. She let the letters form in her mind's eye and fall away as she steeled herself for the lie. Amethyst nodded to herself as they were waved forward by an officer with a very long blond braid that fell down her shoulder.

"Remember, don't talk unless they talk to you," Her mom said under her breath.

"License and registration," the officer asked.

Josh produced the papers from his back pocket.

"Citizenship papers," he asked next.

Her mom took out their papers from the glove box. The officer immediately began shining his long flashlight into each of their faces and comparing them to the passports. He sighed and nodded, perhaps disappointed that he couldn't toss all three of them in the back of his car. "Your face is a little red. Have you been drinking?"

"No, Officer. It's an allergy." Amethyst nodded as he did, mirroring his body language. She could barely see his eyes beyond the shine of the flashlight. All there was, was a thick bar of black space between his nose and the brim of his hat.

"Are you adopted?"

Amethyst was caught off guard by the question, but Arnett nodded, and Amethyst nodded as well.

"Can you scoot over to the window closest to me?" His voice was firm. "And roll down the window for me," he spoke in Josh's direction, his tone less friendly.

He called a man named Cooper over, and he brought with him a small plastic package.

"Put your hand out of the window. I'm just going to prick your finger," he said as he opened the kit.

"Is this really necessary? We have to check in soon," Arnett said more toward the dashboard than to him.

Amethyst got up and sat back down closer to the window; in the new light, she could see his moss green eyes, and he pointed with them, so she took the queue and let her arm somewhat dangle out of the window. Josh didn't look nervous, and Amethyst didn't even look in her mom's direction. She knew this was bad. They were testing her for the gene, and there was no way to stop them.

Their car was surrounded by other cars haphazardly parked in the middle of the biggest highway in the seven unified territories, and in front of and behind them were police. His hands were warm as he positioned her thumb. The prick wasn't light; it was deep, and it stung, and she couldn't even recoil as he squeezed the finger to produce a drop of blood. He sucked it into a small plastic tube and closed it.

"We are now required to send anyone found with the gene to a unified territory so they can deal with the proceedings. It takes about an hour for results, so I'm going to need you to move out of line to the side of the road next to the woman with the long black hair." He smiled as he said this.

"OK, see you in a bit," Josh said as he pulled the car slightly forward and to the side. Josh rolled up Amethyst's window, and in one concentrated blow, he hit the steering wheel.

"I can't do anything beyond this. I'm sorry," Josh said; his voice faltered. "Are you OK, Amethyst?" Josh turned around.

Amethyst wasn't yet affected by what had happened. It didn't fully hit her that she would most likely be arrested. Instead, she felt the small dot of dried blood on her thumb glide over the seats, the rawness of the rash on her cheeks, and the salty air that drifted into the thin strips of the open window. Arnett touched her eyes with her sleeves; Amethyst knew to keep herself from crying. Arnett then began rubbing her legs and squeezing her arms, a skill she learned in therapy when Amethyst was still in upper school after her dad had died.

Cars began driving past, emptying the artery of road behind them and in front of them. One of the checkpoint lights was turned off and, within another thirty minutes, the second one and finally the last one at fifty minutes into their wait for results. It was then, watching the lights dim, that it dawned on her that if they had stopped at the drugstore, they might have missed the checkpoint.

Amethyst let herself cry, the tears burning her cheeks like lava. The officer came over, looking at a big communication device. He tapped on Amethyst's window, and Josh obliged and rolled it down.

"I'm going to need you to come with me," he said, a dark tone to his voice.

"By herself?" Arnett nearly growled at him.

"Yes, she's not a minor in this territory. She's an adult. If you want to reach her, I will give you her number." He spoke plainly.

Amethyst took a deep breath as he opened her car door, the cool air hitting her tears and drying them on contact. There was no time to look back and see her mom again as the officer twisted her arm around her back, pushing her forward toward a parked cruiser on the grass beside the highway in front of their car. Out of the corner of her eye, she could see a man in a red car drive past and crane his neck to look. A moment later, handcuffs were put on, and she felt a warm hand on the top of her head as she was put in the back of the police car.

"We're just going to Central Glass Hill, and from there, Amethyst, we're sending you to Diamond Sea. They will take care of you from there. You are not in any trouble. I'm Officer Blair." He spoke slowly.

"What about my mom?" Amethyst said, suddenly feeling sick.

"That's up to the Authority." Officer Blair began turning some knobs until his radio had a clear signal. The weather report looped until they arrived at the police station.

Glass Hill

Amethyst

Glass Hill was exactly what it sounded like. It was a hilly, skyscraper-covered city in Maykis Isle. It was the one part of the territory that wasn't a maze of office buildings, factories, and labs. TerraTech still owned the majority of the buildings, so crime really didn't happen there. Their crime rate was some ridiculously low number. In the center of the city was a group of four tall, thin skyscrapers, forming a four-part square. Every so often, there was some fancy train station or an ornate water fountain.

The officer didn't speak to Amethyst for the entirety of the trip. It wasn't until they pulled into the parking lot of the Central Glass Hill Precinct that he acknowledged she was still in the car.

The car was surrounded by other cruisers before she was let out. And when she was, a large number of officers formed an unbroken circle around her. Officer Blair didn't explain anything and only kept his hand poised on top of his gun. Inside, Amethyst was taken to a room at the very back of the building; and the whole trip down the hall, she was flanked by officers. She must have looked like a murderer.

The room she was taken to was cool but not cold, and there was food waiting there for her. It was a turkey sandwich, a dark cola, and veggie chips.

"I'll see you later, about twenty minutes. Eat," Officer Blair said as he walked backward out the door. Amethyst was hungry, but she also felt like she was about to throw up. She didn't know if it was related to the rash or being taken. Perhaps it was a little bit of both.

This wasn't what she imagined would happen when she was taken. She always pictured there would be more fighting, more tears, and more yelling, but there was none. The clearest thing was the blinding lights of the cruiser and the cold night air and all the silence. There was so much silence.

She didn't take out her cell phone just in case they take it from her, but man, did she want to. She had no idea what was going on outside her small world, and she would have at least liked to know if her mom and Josh were OK, as OK as they could possibly be.

She opened the sandwich, thinking it would be worth the attempt to eat something. The sandwich was dry, the mayonnaise packet wrapped at the bottom. She opened the chips, hoping the taste would help with her nausea. They weren't salty like she expected. They just tasted like fried air. The drink perked her up though. It soothed away a headache she didn't realize she had.

They moved so fast from the checkpoint to the empty conference room that she lost all sense of time. It must almost be morning, but she wasn't sure, and she was at a poor angle to see the time on the dashboard. She didn't know why she didn't look at the clock when she walked into the precinct; the lack of knowing the time was bothering her.

Officer Blair walked in, and she realized she ran out of time to eat. The sandwich laid there, bread taken off from the top, awaiting the mayo. He was joined by three other male officers, who all had concern etched on their faces, furrowing their brows. "You can take that with you if you like." He waved Amethyst toward the door.

Amethyst was led down a maze of hallways before arriving at an indoor lot. Parked there was one small black van. It didn't look like a police vehicle. It didn't look like anything. She was put in the third row while the other officers sat in front of her, and Officer Blair drove.

As the garage door opened, soft golden rays of sunlight bathed the inside of the driver's seat. The back windows were tinted. She was simply more comfortable knowing it was morning and that the passage of time was far slower in reality than in her imagination. Josh and her mom could not have been too far off. Maybe they were being questioned. It might take days. She couldn't do anything now, but the time wasn't falling away like she thought.

They drove for an hour and ten minutes to an airport. The airport was a small one with only a few airlines, all going in the direction of the Crow Territory. Amethyst wondered if TerraTech had set this all up. Even the planes looked new, and they had names she never heard of like Ink Skies and Turpeek Air. The airport was mostly empty. She saw one group of Crow citizens who, she assumed, was a family by their variety of ages. They took one look at her and muttered something under their breath. The man stared at her as Officer Blair filled out paperwork for her free ticket.

She admitted in her head it must look odd—one girl surrounded by officers with no luggage. She focused on the large, softly ticking analog clock above the ticket counter. Officer Blair took a copy of her real paperwork out of his pocket for the unduly smiling woman and let out a stream of affirmatives as she looked over the paperwork, read some things back to him, and handed him the ticket. He then paid for a ticket for himself and another officer who had the Maykis Isle Police Department logo emblazoned on it. The red-and-gold curved lightning bolts were in a dark green circle.

In the next thought, Amethyst realized it must have been her face they were staring at, and it made her self-conscious. It wasn't as red as it was last night, but it was still there. Her skin wasn't covered with small spots anymore, but the areas where they were before were now slightly raised. She hoped it wasn't permanent.

The flight was almost immediately taking off. It was only her, Officer Blair, the other older officer, and that family who stared at her. She sat between them and resented the seating arrangement the whole ride. She could barely move her legs, let alone rest her eyes. The flight was a long three hours. When they landed, she was escorted only by Officer Blair. The other officer went to the bathroom in the lobby of the airport.

Diamond Sea's airport was just as small as the previous one but more beautiful. A long, unending pane of glass displayed a panoramic view of the body of water in front of them and, on the opposite end, the forest behind them. It did not quite dawn on Amethyst that she was in the Crow Territory immediately. Her eyes realized it first as they watered, sending tears down her checks that stung the rash, and her legs, getting the memo, buckled beneath her. Officer Blair tried to stand her up but stopped as he realized her body was shaking as if it was convulsing. The other officer came back then, visibly concerned, and offered Amethyst water and fanned her with his notepad.

"Maybe we should have her sit," the older officer said as he picked her up like a doll and walked her half-useful legs over to the group of four conjoined chairs. Officer Blair was calling someone. She didn't even notice at first; her breathing seemed to drown out everything happening around her.

They didn't go anywhere for a while. Soon her breathing slowed to a more comfortable pace, but her legs still felt like putty. Neither of them rushed her.

Officer Blair got a text at around four thirty. Amethyst could tell from the notification sound. It was just like hers. He got up from the chair and held out his hand. "Do you think you could walk?" Officer Blair said as he looked at his phone.

Amethyst thought about this. If she said she could, then she would immediately be taken to wherever it was she was going; but if she said no, she'd probably be looked over at a hospital, suspected sick or something, and it would only prolong everything. She was tired. Her chest hurt, and she felt dizzy, and she knew from personal experience this was all anxiety. It was over for now, but she didn't want to risk another episode by letting her mind wander, thinking up all these scenarios swirling around her head with each tick of the clock. The longer she waited, the bigger this would become. She nodded, and he helped her up.

She was taken to parking lot C and walked to a large SUV. She didn't know what to expect. They waited for a moment and then another moment and finally one more until the darkly tinted window was rolled down. Sitting in the driver's seat was a tall woman who looked a lot like Amethyst. She had honey-colored skin, long dark brown hair, and a ruddy complexion to her cheeks. Her eyes were obscured behind shades. But there was no mistaking the slightly round, angled jaw and dimpled chin. Her hair was graying.

Officer Blair was gawking at this woman, especially as her legs emerged from the SUV. They were long and barely covered. She opened the back seat and said nothing. Amethyst didn't get in right away, and as she did, Officer Blair handed her some paperwork. "This is your identification number. Your adoptive mother has been given the same one. She'll be able to contact you. Good luck." And he nodded and turned, slowly walking away.

The woman was silent for a moment and seemed to be sizing Amethyst up. It made her nervous. "You've grown, little sister," the woman said. She put her hand on Amethyst's thighs, lightly patting them. The car smelled strongly of whatever perfume she used, and on the dashboard was a thick file, and Amethyst wondered if it was about her.

So this wasn't her mom. She wondered silently about what it meant.

"You haven't said anything. You must be tired. You can talk when we get back to the house. There are a few people who want to see you. I'm Zircon. I'm your eldest sister by eight years." She placed her hand on top of hers.

"I'm gonna close the door, OK?" Zircon nodded yes to Amethyst, who was glad she asked. The past day and a half was doors unceremoniously shut after a moment of speech. The drive wasn't long, and thankfully, it was quiet.

Zircon removed her shades, revealing dark gray eyes. It caught Amethyst off guard. She seemed kind enough. She didn't try to pry any information from her but continued to talk, looking periodically in the rearview mirror to get a good look at her face.

"You were sent sometime around your second birthday. I remember this acutely. I helped Mom bake the cake. She wouldn't let me put it in the stove, but she did let me frost it." She sped a little to get past a leisurely car. "I think we still have some of your things. Lorelei saved them from Mom. She didn't want to remember too much. The wait was really long for you." She paused to drink water from a silver water bottle. "Don't mention that. I didn't tell you that." She shook her head and smiled. She didn't continue talking but focused on the back road she was going down.

Amethyst was slowly processing that she had another life, one that she didn't remember but was no less significant for the people who knew who she was and her parents. Zircon spoke without filling in the blanks of who Lorelei was and what their mother's name was as if she should just know. It annoyed her, but what does one do in this kind of situation? Zircon basically had to reteach her how to butter a piece of toast to a person who had no concept of toast.

"Was your named changed?"

"No, I don't think so. It's Amethyst."

"You can call them if you like. Do you have a cell phone?"

"No, I don't. It was left in the car." Amethyst didn't know why she lied and why her tone was so off. She realized then she was holding on to her pants as if they would be ripped out from under her; she was clawing at them so bad.

"We're almost there."

❧

The house was covered in gray stone and ivy. It had to be really old. On the right side of the house was a moon gate that led to a little pond. The only car parked there was a huge SUV, and it looked so out of place. The house was fresh out of a fairy tale. And it was not complete without billions of delicate, colorful flowers edging the pathway to it. The only thing that was missing was a few bunny rabbits and the song of chirping birds. Something about it made Amethyst angry.

Zircon opened her door, helping Amethyst down as if she was helpless. It didn't change as they walked inside because she immediately began to usher her to sit and rest. The house was minimally decorated. In the center of the living room were a three-seater sofa, a television, and a large gold hexagon coffee table, and underneath was a large gray rug that filled most of the floor space. In the left-hand corner was a wooden staircase with plexiglass railings. After Zircon brought her a jug of water and a glass, she stopped hovering and went into the kitchen to cook. It was down one long hallway, so it was doubtful her voice would carry, and as a consequence, there was no conversation.

The house smelled distinctly of cinnamon and sugar. Maybe it was a candle. There were little objects on the mantel below the TV, but she didn't study them. All she could focus on was the little square of concentrated blue light in her pocket and texting anyone outside this fresh hell. The house smelled wrong, the couch felt wrong, and the air had an odd quality.

She felt for it just to make sure it was still there. Slowly, she took it out, turned on the screen, and let out a deep sigh when the battery life indicated there was still 60 percent. A pile of messages appeared on her screen, all from her mom. She skimmed them and learned that the Authority was still deciding what to do, but it was likely they were going to fine them for each falsified document. She said they weren't arrested, and no one had talked to them about what happened. She read they drove back to the Bluebird Territory and split up at Moss Point, and Arnett began researching about the laws in the Crow Territory and said she wouldn't be able to bring her back because, according to the new laws, she would be seen in the Crow Territory as a minor for four years. It was all to keep her there, and the thought made her sink deeper into the couch.

Zircon emerged, and Amethyst realized she didn't know how long she was standing there. Zircon walked over slowly and spoke each sentence like she was reciting a poem. "You really can call. I won't stop you."

"I wouldn't even know where to start. I know it probably seems so easy to you, all this, but for me, it's not."

"It's not a jail sentence. You can still call your adoptive mom and your friends. We just need you here." Zircon emphasized *here* and walked so close that she was just a foot away from the sofa, her hands poised at her sides. She touched her cheek, the skin still raised though no longer red. She sat on the coffee table, and her disposition had changed.

Zircon looked to be deep in thought, and when she arrived at the thought, it irritated her so much that the side of her face twitched as a frown appeared. Whatever she was searching for in Amethyst's face wasn't there.

In the moment, Amethyst only felt the pull of the weight that seemed to accumulate in her heart and head. She felt something stuck in her throat.

"How long have you had this rash?"

"What?"

"How long?"

"A few days. Why?"

Flat

Zora

The touch wasn't particularly abrasive, but it was noticeable. The prick happened in a split second, but the warm feeling was luscious. It covered Zora from each follicle to every vein. Nothing was explained to her, but that didn't matter to her. All she wanted was to forget. She knew she was given a drug every morning and at night. And once a week, an injection in her arm made a deep, warm feeling race all over her body. It felt like being hugged from the inside. It felt like being dipped into soup. It felt like sex. She looked forward to the time at night where she could close her eyes and let the feeling envelop her.

The drugs made her feel hazy, and she liked the feeling, even more than she liked not thinking about what happened. The more days passed, the more she could vaguely remember what had happened that night the Authority came to her apartment. Every night she would recite what she needed to remember. Her name and her age were all she really needed to know, but she added other things about herself so she wouldn't be completely lost to the fog.

Her name was Zora June Jo'nest, her age was twenty years, her favorite color was mint, and her mother's name was Erma Patel, and today was April 20. Every so often, the people who visited her told her the name of another woman named Eliza, but she learned to place the name in the back of her mind and not think of it when the drugs wore off around midday and in the middle of the night. If she thought of it while the drugs were swimming around, she was more likely to remember.

One night, angry, she remembered Sasha, and now she couldn't get his face out of her head. His voice, his scent, even the navy blue button-down he sometimes wore seemed to live on every surface of her closet of a room. Each day she would try to replace the thought of him with anything else. A week ago, she found a salamander on a windowsill, and she imagined that it had an intricate pattern, like plaid or houndstooth, and its eyes were stripped. It didn't take long for her to dream about it, and she was grateful when she dreamed about this and not being under Sasha.

The Band-Aid was placed on the small speck of blood, and she was waved to the side for the next person. Everyone's reaction was the same—a wince, a grimace, and then a long, deep sigh. Standing up, she could feel the heat traveling down her body like the stream of a hot shower. This would last all day. Eating came next, but this was never easy as the drug suppressed all feelings, especially appetite.

The meal was only a sandwich and an apple as it was lunch, and Zora, now more attuned to this song and dance, chewed as she knew the more she did an action, the more natural it would feel. She didn't know anyone here. People would come and go, and the people who stayed for a while, like herself, were moved to other halls and assigned to other mess halls. Days slipped away too, especially the earlier ones when she just arrived. The Authority overdosed newbies until they seemed to be settled. Zora wondered if her memories would return or be lost forever if she stopped taking the drug.

The alarm went off to signal that lunch was over, and she stood to be counted, like everybody, with a click. They were then sent to the open courtyard to get an hour of sunlight. It was the only part of the compound that Zora thought was pretty, just pretty, though, not beautiful. There was a fountain in the center that went off every ten minutes; after six of them, they would go back to their rooms to watch time fall away until dinner. And this was just how it was. It was a circle of eating, taking drugs, and sleeping.

In the courtyard, she had a bench she liked to sit in when it was empty and watch the bees try to find hospitable flowers. Her life wasn't going in any particular direction, so it was nice to see something moving forward. She had watched tulips grow from the bulbs the groundskeepers planted a while ago, and now chubby bees were burying themselves in them.

In the soft light of the sun, she could pretend for the hour to be back in the Bluebird Territory in the city center, Muse rambling in her ear as they went for coffee at Kirk's. These dates weren't planned. Muse often ran into her as she was walking Dancer, but she didn't totally dislike them either. Zora didn't know why it was this memory that seemed so crisp. Sometimes these memories made her cry and not like an emotional cry but almost like a reflex. She didn't feel sad.

She watched people walk loops around the fountain in small groups and the breeze bend grass and cattails at the other end of the courtyard. She watched a girl rake her shoe over pulverized pebbles at the edge of the stairs and twirl her hand around her auburn hair. She watched a boy, much younger than her, cry, sitting under a tree that was just sprouting. She breathed in the scent of maple and cut grass and felt the warmth of the metal bars underneath her.

Three long, graceful sprouts of water created *U*s that crisscrossed underneath one another and then fell hard against the granite circle at the bottom. Only five more.

She tried to pretend they didn't exist, but every so often, they would come away from the periphery of her vision and walk over to one of the kids who seemed especially low or even angry. Those were not normal reactions here. They wore all-black, formfitting suits (possibly Lycra) and tall boots. It was hard to tell them apart sometimes because they all wore black masks across their eyes. The almond-shaped openings combined with the somewhat thick strip of fabric made differentiating people by their eyes hard, especially the men. They didn't wear name tags, and Zora always thought that to be sketchy.

When she arrived, there was one man who scared her in particular, but he looked like a few other men, and she found herself constantly afraid. She knew he didn't do anything out of the ordinary to her, illegal or otherwise, but there was something particularly dark about how he spoke to her, how he asked her to do things, and how he grabbed her from her bed when she didn't want to wake up the first morning she found herself at the compound.

It was easier to just pretend none of them existed. They usually stood around the courtyard walls and the mess hall and to the entrance to every set of rooms. They weren't watching for people trying to escape, she realized. They were watching for the effect the drugs were having. Sometimes if you seemed happy or sad or angry to a high degree, you were given a small white pill to flatten that feeling. It had only happened to Zora once.

She was in her room, making her bed, and something inside her faltered. She cried as she tore off the sheets, and she couldn't finish the task. Her eyes were clouded with tears. A soft knock then followed, and three of them were standing outside her door. The one in the center handed her the pill, and wanting to stop the achy feeling, she took it. Now this extra dose didn't just gracefully announce its entrance; it stormed through and threw down its bags in the center of your skull. She spent the rest of the day resting, and no one bothered her.

The boy sitting under the tree was offered a pill, and he took it. The woman with long blond hair who offered it walked back to her station at the corner of the stairs.

Zora stood up and began walking around the fountain. She did this until the alarm went off to go back to the rooms. From this point, they just allowed them to walk back on their own. None of the doors were locked. On her way back, she stopped by a man and was taken instead to the offices that were in a heavily guarded wing accessed only with key cards and finger scans.

While the other parts of the compound looked like an old boarding school, this wing looked like a modern office complete with glass desks and windows that touched the floor and ceiling. She was taken to room B, and in front of her was someone from the Authority. He said nothing to her as she sat but pushed in front of her a heavy file that was spilling with pictures of the mall. "I'm going to need you to give a statement about what happened in the mall," he said, taking a pad of paper out of his jacket pocket.

"I already gave a statement. You should have just recorded me the day I came. I put in the code that belonged to my mom. I did it. We all know it." Zora's voice was flat.

"There's no evidence of that."

There wouldn't be, she thought. They just had to take her word for it. She had disarmed the security to trigger the explosion. What she had done wouldn't show up in any of the logs. She made sure of that.

She hadn't thought of that afternoon in a long time. She was still stuck on the night she was taken from her bed and pulled into the hallway. They sped through her rights and put on the handcuffs so fast that she didn't catch what she was being arrested for, and now they couldn't prove what she did, not that it would change her situation, but it did put part of it in limbo. On one side was this circle of being questioned, and on the other was jail time and getting her rights as an adult stripped away and put into a strange woman's custody. Maybe this was just a game. Maybe they wanted to just further incriminate her with the information they gathered from her frustration. She didn't know.

"We only know you were there, but that is not enough to prove you did it. We can place you in the control room before and after it happened, but we need to know exactly how you found the code. That information is not easy to access. You're an economics major. This isn't your realm." A soft smile appeared on his face then as he pulled out a pen.

"The code was written on an old piece of mail." She really didn't remember what it was written on, only that it was a piece of paper in her mother's closet.

"Can you recall the code if asked?"

"No, I don't remember it at all."

"That's fine." He began writing.

"What were the steps to disarming the system? Would you be able to do it if we brought you a computer?"

"I don't remember. All I know is it was more than seven steps." It was the most distinct thing she remembered. She had to run through all the steps in her head before the day of execution because she kept forgetting or missing a step. To miss a step meant the police would be called to the control room and would have her arrested then and there.

"Was anyone with you in the room?"

"No." But the truth was she wasn't sure either way. A girl named Roe had helped her figure out the security system, but she wasn't going to dispense that name until all hope was lost. There was no point in roping her into this.

"What do you remember about the control room? Can you describe it?"

"It was a black room with a large touch screen panel on the wall and a screen that swiveled in the corner. There was gray carpet." There was more she remembered, but she was getting sleepy, the drug now deeper in her system.

"We'll talk tomorrow." He left, and the guards of the campus showed up to escort her back to her room.

In her room, she slept until dinner when one of them woke her up for her next dose.

Cerplex

Sasha

The only contact his dad had with Sasha since Zora and Muse were arrested was telling him the people who destroyed his windows were arrested and to arrange to have the windows fixed. They were repaired within twenty-four hours.

It had been nearly two weeks, and the boards were of no help. It was all about a small, inconsequential protest on April 15 that triggered nothing and incriminated no one. Sasha tried his best to keep up appearances and show up to a few, but it was only him as everyone else did not trust to stand near him. He decided to lie low after his third protest when the board mentioned him by name. He didn't have the time to repair another broken window or explain to the landlord what was happening. His last name was enough for the landlord to let it go because all that Ashford translated to was money to fix whatever was wrong.

As of now, he was sitting in his living room, paging through a clothing catalog, thinking about how much he wanted to spend. He needed clothes not out of necessity but to help distance himself from himself. If the style was different enough, maybe he could fly under the radar. He guessed it would be simpler if he just found another apartment, but just how far he was willing to go he didn't know.

Everything was more or less central in the Bluebird Territory, especially in the city center. He opened his banking app, saw it had increased by a couple of thousand, and closed it again. He wanted all the money that wasn't typically gone. If it was gone, he wouldn't have to think about how he got it; at least that was what he hoped would happen. It amounted to four thousand per person he had built a case that led to arrest, which was, at current count, seven. The amount he got for Zora and Muse was higher. He decided to replace some of his furniture. That was expensive. That would get rid of a chuck of the money.

He got up from the couch and looked around the room as if it would give him the inspiration. He didn't pick out any of the furniture he currently had. His father did. He didn't even technically rent the apartment; it belonged to his father. He then wondered how expensive it would be to replace more or less everything in the apartment—a fresh start.

Just as these ideas were swimming around his brain, his dad called. "Yeah."

"I'm going to need you to come into the lab. We have a few doses ready."

"I'm a little busy right now."

"It's only a pill. It won't put you on your ass. Maykis Labs developed a new, kinder formula. How are you feeling?"

"Fine, never better."

"Any new skin rashes?"

"No, is that happening?"

"To some, yes. I don't want it to hit you while you're in the streets and be tested under suspicion. Come in. It'll take thirty minutes."

"Give me an hour. I have to shower."

Hakeem escorted him to the lab in his navy blue convertible. The sun was beginning to come out, and the streets were covered in crushed petals from the first signal of spring. The security gate was now requiring three types of identification, in addition to a vocal invite via phone call from someone within the building. The process ate up twenty of the thirty minutes his dad promised the whole process would take. The lab was filled with people, and his dad was in the goldfish bowl on a phone call. Hakeem pushed him forward, waving his pass card that opened the door to the office.

Marcus hung up the phone and began cleaning off his desk so he could place a tray he had prepped with the drug—another injection and a pill. "Low-dose Cerplex was found to slow down the transformation process by six months. We're developing another drug for the long term.

But for now, two pills in a weekly injection is what it required. We'll try this regimen for a month, take some blood, and see how much the gene was suppressed. It's almost like a cancer." He stood up from his desk and washed his hands, gloved, and sat next to Sasha on a metal stool.

"Cerplex is that mind-control drug that prisoners are given."

"As well as those with anxiety and depression. It's complicated, but whatever it is, there's something in the mind that triggers the message in the body to start transforming. Cerplex slows down this message. It's like shutting off puberty."

Sasha remembered the pain of when the gene was suppressed for him, and if that wasn't the last of it, he'd do what he had to so he did not have to experience it again. He only nodded, and the injection was delivered squarely to his shoulder. It felt warm, almost hot. There was a flood of hot blood filling his cheeks and his hands. The pill, on the other hand, was like a battering ram.

"The medication, once it is in your system, leaves you somewhat suggestable, so avoid focusing on anything too long. I'll have Regina come by and check on you periodically." He touched Sasha's head. That, too, felt warm. His whole body felt like it was swimming.

"Avoid sex, rich foods, and spending large sums of money. You can become addicted to the rush of serotonin on this drug."

"Yes, I'm going to do that." Sasha laughed.

They didn't laugh.

The ride back was silent, and he was grateful of this because every part of his body felt like it was under warm water. He could only focus on this feeling. He was given a bottle of pills to take twice a day, and Regina would later next week show him how to inject himself. That night he had the best sleep he had in a long time.

Salve

Amethyst

Amethyst was sitting at the kitchen table as Zircon rubbed a green cream on her cheeks, which cooled her down on contact. "It won't fix exactly what is wrong, but it buys us some time to fix the situation. I'll let Mom explain what is happening." Zircon shook her head. "I want you to understand this isn't done for pride or vanity but necessity. It would be wrong to let you experience this pain much longer." Zircon got up from the chair in front of her and started rubbing the cream along her eyelids and the excess on her forehead and neck.

"What can you do for me that doctors cannot? I've had the pain for years. I'm obviously sick."

"You're not sick at all. You just don't belong in the Bluebird Territory. It's what is making you sick. I'll let Mom explain. I texted her this morning. She should be here soon."

Zircon didn't let her respond as she left the kitchen and went to the room that adjoined it. She came back with her cell phone and set it beside her on the kitchen table. "How does your face feel?"

"It doesn't sting."

Zircon smiled and, taking on a reciting-like tone, said, "It's silver flower root. It only grows here."

Amethyst couldn't think of what else to say at first. In the hour she saw her rash, she did more to help her than her real mom was able to. The rash felt like it had disappeared, and all the pain was now gone. She wanted to know what could be making her sick in the Bluebird Territory. She knew there was a mutated gene that they tested for, but there was never any explanation on why only Crow adoptees had this gene. It was just treated as an illness; sometimes it was given a name that matched some of the symptoms of a well-known illness, but often only the symptoms were treated.

Amethyst knew firsthand what it was like to only have the symptoms treated or downplayed. One afternoon, in the middle of her bio lab, she began experiencing the most intense pain in her stomach and legs. She was bent over in tears, and after an hour of being moved to the sick bay and having paramedics show up, she was asked if she was on her period—those exact words.

Zircon was already up and moving around again before Amethyst could come back at her with her questions. She seemed nervous, and that made Amethyst nervous. In fluid motions, Zircon put the remainder of the salve in a jar and twisted the lid on tight. She began to boil a pot of water on the stove in the next moment. "Do you have a preference on how you like your chicken?"

Amethyst shook her head and watched as Zircon began seasoning the pot of water in front of her, using small, short containers on a large carousel on the counter. "Why is this happening?" Amethyst gestured around her face, her fingers trailing around the bumps on her face.

"It's really complicated, and the best way I can tell you what is going on is to show you what is happening. I can't do it on my own, so once Mom is done in her garden, she'll come, and it will all make sense. It's far complicated to be believed." Zircon mumbled her words over the pot of water that was beginning to boil. She wasn't going to answer any of her questions, and it was starting to give her a headache how the conversation went in a circle with no resolution other than to wait.

❧

Over a pot of tea, they ate chicken in the slowly fading light of the enclosed patio at the back of the house. Zircon pointed out the flowers that were growing in her raised garden beds and pointed out the song of robins that flew from one tree to another. The patio faced a small beach inlet and families of jagged rocks that formed a scalloped edge. Cattails swayed with the wind in a wild dance as the water was pulled in and out. Amethyst didn't have much to say because Zircon talked a lot about the flora and fauna of Diamond Sea and spoke nothing about her biological mom. Toward the end of the night, Zircon monitored her phone, Amethyst guessed for text messages.

"Did you have any close friends in the Bluebird Territory?" Zircon said after flipping up her phone to look at the screen.

"I had one, two . . . Sasha and Muse. We usually spent time together on the weekends. Sasha I knew since high school. Muse was more of his friend though," Amethyst said as she chewed a small bit of rice, looking down at her plate. Once the food was gone, there would only be more awkward conversation. She wouldn't be able to piecemeal the conversation. She took small bites of chicken and rice here and there, making an effort to perfect every forkful of food.

Zircon got a text, and this was indicated by a sparkly wind chime sound that reverberated in the air. As she read the text, her eyes seemed to dart back and forth; she nodded to the text before actually answering it, and then her fingers were off, dancing across the keyboard at a speed that impressed Amethyst. "She's on her way. You want to go back to the living room?"

"Yeah, sure." The food was already cold, so there was no reason to continue this forced eating.

They returned to the living room, and Zircon walked over to the mantel, revealing a small radio concealed behind a stack of books. She played some easy listening and sat on the arm of the chair, watching Amethyst intently. "I want you to be comfortable here. If there's anything you need, just let me know. Do you need some privacy?" Zircon said softly, concern marking her features.

Amethyst did want privacy, but she didn't believe that was at all possible in a house that was strange to her. There was nothing but to wait for her biologically mother, which was a prospect that tightened every tendon in her body. It was like waiting for a Band-Aid to be pulled off; she winced at the thought, but she just wanted it done. She wanted it to happen so fast that she didn't have time to think, but that wasn't happening. "I'm fine here," Amethyst lied.

In that moment, she thought about her mom, who was somewhere in the five territories, most likely wondering how she was and wondering what legal action they were going to take. She wondered how Josh was taking everything, and she hoped not too hard. It wasn't his fault they were caught, and Amethyst hoped he knew that. They took such a roundabout route; it was odd that the checkpoints were there for so long.

Amethyst was only angry at the Crow government. They were the ones who decided it was OK to rip families apart. They made it legal. People would do all kinds of things, both good and bad, just so long as it was deemed legal. She didn't realize how her thoughts were affecting her face because Zircon looked even more concerned.

"I'm sorry," Amethyst said into her folded hands. She didn't know what exactly she was apologizing for, but it couldn't make things worse than they already were at the moment.

Outside, the sound of pebbles crunching below tires stalled all that was happening in the living room. Zircon stood up, poised in front of the chair, before gracefully walking over to the door. Amethyst didn't want to look. She would rather prolong it. The longer she didn't see this woman, the less real it all seemed.

The door opened, and a deep warm chuckle floated into the air. "Dear," she said, her voice warm and inviting. Zircon walked closer to the threshold in what may have been a hug that migrated back into the house. The door fell behind them.

The woman walked over; the soft click of low heels marked her steps. Amethyst only saw a long, flowing brown skirt decorated with small gold beads. She wore a long macrame belt that cinched the waist of the skirt. Amethyst didn't want to look up. The woman just stood there, her weathered hands painted with raised veins and sunspots. She was patient and did not push Amethyst to do anything.

After a moment, she sat and folded her hands in her lap. From there, she could see the resemblance. Her eyes were a deep color that Amethyst could not name, but her skin was fairer than both the sisters. She had a confident sideways smile that produced a dimple on her right cheek and also a prominent nose piercing on her right nostril that was copper colored. She didn't say anything, only watched the expressions that came across Amethyst's face.

This wasn't what Amethyst was expecting her biological mom to be like. She wasn't sure what she was expecting. In the corner of her eyes, she could see Zircon still standing near the door, watching them both look at each other. The draft from outside was coming in until she locked the door. The outside smelled nice. Amethyst wanted to be outside.

"You're so beautiful, Amethyst," the woman said as he swept her hair behind her ears.

Amethyst didn't say anything. She wasn't good with compliments in the first place, not that this woman would know that. So she did what she always did—nod yes and smile.

"Have you eaten?"

"Yeah, yes, I have. Zircon made chicken." It was that easy to have a conversation. She was surprised.

"Good, good . . . how are you feeling?"

"Fine." This wasn't exactly a lie; it was close enough to the truth for the current level of the relationship.

"Tomorrow we're going to a special place in Diamond Sea. It should help you."

Amethyst didn't like the sound of "should help." She wanted whatever was wrong off her face as soon as possible. She didn't want to experience the kind of blindsiding pain she had been experiencing ever again either.

"I don't know where to start. How long have you been experiencing stomach pain?"

"On and off for three years, more frequently this past month." Amethyst tried to keep a measured tone. Thinking about how long she had been experiencing the pain made her angry. It brought up every doctor appointment to the forefront of her mind again.

"That's a long time," the woman said before she made a quick gesture with her hands as if to say sorry for the what she said. "I mean, it's unusual for the process to take that long. A year perhaps, but if it doesn't occur within the time frame, it goes dormant and doesn't usually resurface as skin rashes." She stood from the couch, her body slightly bent forward, looking at the rash on her face; her hand hovered in the air, tracing over the bumps. "Have you ever had a rash like this before?"

"No." Amethyst didn't mean to sound curt, but she didn't want to diminish how much she was tired of all this either. If she had poster board and a big fat marker, she would make a sign.

"Good, good. I want to touch your skin if that's all right," she said as she stood even closer, her waist at eye level. Her finger touched the surface of Amethyst's skin before she could give the go-ahead. Her hands were warm and smelled like lavender. The touch didn't hurt a lot, but it was uncomfortable when she pressed. It was like a large, thinned pimple on the surface of her skin, and the taut areas felt especially sore. It felt better though. Whatever that green stuff was made out of relieved much of the stinging.

"We'll go early in the morning, OK?" She now held Amethyst's face in her hands, brushing her hair back from around her cheeks. The way she spoke the words was comforting. Though Amethyst didn't get any immediate answers, it was nice having a plan for something. There was nothing more that could be done to her that wasn't already. All her fears were realized, and she was in the Crow Territory with literal strangers. She wouldn't be able to go home immediately. *But* there was a plan to end the pain she was feeling, and inside her, she felt a twinge of excitement building in the pit of her stomach.

"I'm Judy. You can call me Judy. You don't have to call me Mom." She knelt as she said this. It sounded like it hurt her to say this as she frowned yet nodded, her graying hair bobbing around her round face.

Amethyst was thankful when the conversation shifted to Judy and Zircon catching up, talking about people she didn't know, making it so she had nothing to add, relieving her of any required participation. They moved to the kitchen, and she could smell the familiar scent of the green salve Zircon had made earlier, only stronger. They returned with a jar, a darker green this time, and told Amethyst to rub more on her face. She did so and noticed the bumps were beginning to go away, along with the tight feeling. Her face felt back to normal, and it was in this moment that she couldn't help but cry. She didn't understand any of it and was too afraid to ask about any of it.

TRIAL

Marcus

Marcus found himself a little buzzed waiting for the pizza to be delivered. He sat on the couch in his bedroom, staring down at his socks resting inside his shoes. Sasha would be in bed by now, so there was no point in talking to him about what was passed around via the grapevine of protesters.

There was going to be a large demonstration in the auditorium of the high school he had gone to. Marcus understood the significance. It was the same place where the principal told all those students at the age of fourteen to eighteen that they could potentially be one of these children. Some of them already knew and were suspended in a state a shock over the possibility of being sent back. And others like Sasha were angry, regarding it as the ultimate betrayal. Marcus adopted Sasha at three. He hoped Sasha would remember it to make it easier on him in the future, but he had no idea what happened to Sasha before he was delivered to his doorstep.

In the beginning of the famine, it was easy to adopt one of the children. There were no fees, just mountains of paperwork, and especially childless couples adopted most of the children in waiting within the first year of the program. There was a long line in the courthouse to finalize adoption of these children day after day. Sasha wasn't a child anymore.

Marcus realized this. He was beginning to tower over him, and his voice was nearly as deep as his. And if he was diligent, he could grow a beard. He was no longer the toddler he adopted seventeen years ago.

All that was on his mind; this night was about whether Sasha would actually listen this time. He never really did, at least not exactly. Marcus told him to protest and get information, and Sasha slept around and got too involved instead. Marcus told him to take a list of student names and get information, and Sasha enrolled in a class to impress a girl. Now this wasn't the worse thing he had ever done, but it did cause him to lose his focus.

Marcus admitted to himself that Sasha, if he didn't have a name or two in the next two days, had to find another person to do the job. There were three contenders, all of them the children of top researchers. Marcus always thought the ingredient that made Sasha less focused on the task was his knowledge that he was a Lost Child, and he suspected, especially after the corn husk doll incident, that he actually believed in their so-called cause.

Marcus stood after realizing he was sitting for nearly twenty minutes. He walked back to the kitchen, glanced at the communication pad next to the front door, and saw no notifications. The pizza was taking a while.

Covering the table were files of all the Lost Children who were either at the Turpeek campus or on their way there. He didn't keep up with all the kids who went there, but he did like knowing that some in particular were being put in their place. Zora was already receiving treatment, and Muse would start soon. Those two, combined with the 155 who were already sent, should provide enough data on how effective the treatment was in suppressing the mutated gene. The thought of all the data that would be delivered to his doorstep in a few days' time made him giddy.

The only stain in all this was not knowing where Amethyst had gone. One of two things could have happened: either she successfully escaped to the ununified territories or the Crow Territory got to her first. Amethyst was an outlier. She had the gene, but the process started and stopped over years. He would have liked to get his hands on her or, at the very least, some of her blood. Whatever her body was doing with the gene was more effective than the treatment Sasha had, and it would just be perfect if he was able to develop that treatment for Sasha.

His thoughts were stopped by the sound of a soft ping from the communication screen by the door. All he could do in that next hour was rest and eat.

It was nearly two in the morning, and he had spent the better part of the night in the goldfish bowl, looking at a pile of biometric data from many of the kids at Turpeek. Their heart and breathing rates were brought down to normal ranges as the treatment progressed before stabilizing after two weeks. He thought about this while chewing. Their heart rates sometimes sped as if they were doing a vigorous exercise or very sick, but outwardly, at least most of the time, it didn't look as such. They slept for a normal amount of hours, they didn't have any difficulty breathing, and they were as active as any normal young adults. The only oddity was the seemingly random bouts of pain, usually gastrointestinal distress and occasional rashes. It would be easy to just label them with stomach issues if they weren't dying six months to two years after displaying symptoms. The only commonality was they were all from the Crow Territory. The illness was relentless.

The first drug he made, he remembered being so proud of it. It was still under clinical trials when he gave it to Sasha, but it was effective. His pain, after three doses of the drug, was gone. Marcus still didn't trust that it was the end of it because—and he wouldn't tell Sasha this—there were still kids of his age group who died shortly after the trial. It only worked for some of them. He didn't want to think of the number because it made both his heart and head hurt, but it was in the ballpark that six hundred Lost Children had passed. They restarted the trails after the third child who died. Her name was Mazie. She was sixteen.

The beer was beginning to wear off, making his headache from exhaustion more noticeable. He knew he should go to bed, but he couldn't quiet his thoughts. Last year when the anniversary of Sasha's treatment passed, he was fine, but they were coming up on three years in a day. He was eating his fourth pizza at the kitchen island this week, not sitting, his entire body restless.

He thought about the trial over and over again. The weight of the data, hot off the printer, was in his hands. He was walking into the conference room to sort it and then got a call after call from parents who were top officials who had children in the trial and endless text and news alerts from the hospital, school gyms, malls, and cafés. They collapsed. They collapsed and didn't wake up. If they could make it four months without issue in this trial, then he would allow himself to breathe.

TURPEEK

Muse

The van was mostly empty with the exception of them. The sun was beginning to rise, throwing long gold threads of light across the hot leather seats. The driver asked them a few questions, Muse guessed, to make it seem less like a drive to a certifiable prison. He asked them what school they went to, their ages, if they had ever vacationed at Kinder Pond. Muse didn't answer any of them, and the girl Julie answered all of them.

Muse spent most of the drive unraveling the embroidery floss from her hair to distract herself from the cramping in her stomach. Muse didn't have any pads, and she hoped that it wasn't what she thought. Muse would count; each time she saw the large yellow and black sign for Turpeek that announced how many more miles they had left to go. They would be there soon, and she couldn't explain it, but she felt very little behind the thought. She didn't have time to prepare herself for the possibility that she could be taken and sent back. She always thought there would be more time, that the situation would die down, and that one morning she would wake up groggy and, in her half-awake state, read a headline on her communicator that a law was put in place that would make it illegal for the Crow Territory to take literal adults back to their biological parents. She felt it building when she thought about it.

She was twenty-one. She wasn't a child. The only reason she still was living with her adopted mom was it offered her some level of legal protection to stay with her—well, that was until they started the program of sending back "enemies of the state," which really meant student protesters. Living with her mom had meant if she did something illegal, her mother would get a fine as opposed to Muse being sent to jail. Muse saved for these potentialities. She had three part-time jobs for her war fund. The corn husk doll situation cost her nearly five thousand out of the eight she had. But it didn't matter anymore because all that money would be seized shortly after they took her.

It was only four hours ago; she was sitting in the park with her mom and Dancer, walking him for Zora's mom, that a group of woman from the Authority surrounded them. They asked for her paperwork, which she now always kept on her, and after a scan of the seal, they pulled her up and zip-tied her hands behind back and pulled her onto her ass. The pain of being slammed down like that was exquisite. It went up her spine and was concentrated on her right ribs because, as they pulled her, she couldn't help but go into a hunched, half-kneeling position. Muse couldn't look at her mom, who was asking repeatedly what was going on and not given an answer. It was, for all intents and purposes, a kidnapping rather than arrest. She wasn't arrested; she was being taken. She didn't have any rights anymore.

They began to slow down, and in the left side of the van, she could see them turning down a long road. At first, there was nothing much to look at but overgrown grass, cattails, and marshes. But after a few moments, she saw a sand-colored building pull into view. It looked like a school. On the right side of it, she could see tall wire gates and red-banded black cameras. The windows were long, thin slits at the top and large at the bottom that wrapped around it. She could see inside an office. Maybe it was a precinct, but then why the gates?

They pulled into a lot on the left side of the building that was similarly gated right after they drove through. The doors quickly opened on both sides, and they were given no time to acclimate or even ready their bodies to get down before they were being shouted at to disembark. They were pulled inside and taken down a long hall of rooms, past the mess hall, and into the front of the building to the office area. They were weighed and fingerprinted and then taken to room B.

A video was starting, showing an aerial view of the compound the same way they walked down the halls, and a member of the Authority appeared. Muse's head was bowed. She felt the hot tears drip from her face onto her folded hands. The other girl loudly laughed. It made Muse jump.

"Welcome to Turpeek Compound. Here, you will participate in the clinical trial designed to lessen the severity of gene 8alpha6."

Muse stopped paying attention after that and only felt her entire body tense up. Her cramps now worse, she laid her head on the table and prayed they would end soon. The video wasn't long, but the music in the background made her head hurt. They were taken from the room right when the video ended and put into separate rooms. Muse lay down immediately upon the opportunity.

Fog

Sasha

Sasha woke up with a headache. Even the sound of the rain and the cool, damp air that was drifting from the opened window made his body ache. He took his next dose and went to eat breakfast. The café was nearly empty, probably less people wanting to walk in the rain. He looked over the shoulder of the guy in front of him; the glass case of breakfast sandwiches was full. He knew immediately that bacon would be a no-go, just like ham, egg, and cheese should be OK.

He ate his sandwich as he waited for his coffee. Watching the rain grow to a torrential rate, he began to think about how much water was being dumped onto cars and into the gutter. This thought spun around in his head over and over as he grabbed his coffee from the small wooden box, walked down the block, went into the lobby, and pressed the button in the elevator. Sasha couldn't help but watch the rain build up on the small shelf formed by the joining of the windowpanes, overflow, and drip down to the ledge. He sat there for an hour, moved only by the sound of his phone on the kitchen island buzzing and shifting on the granite.

It was his dad calling and no text. Sasha called, put it on speaker, and watched the rain from his peripheral vision. He picked up immediately.

"Have you taken—"

"Yes, 9:40 a.m."

"Good, I want you to take note of when you take each dose. Treat this as scientifically as possible."

"I will. I had a headache this morning, and I've been thinking a lot about the rain. I can't stop watching it."

"Well, the rain is really coming down, but if you find yourself having a thought, don't think about it too long. It's really easy for you to hyperfixate on things in this state."

"How do I not think about things?"

"Time yourself. If the thought doesn't end in a minute or so, focus on something else. Think of a host of things at once. Name the things in your apartment."

Sasha didn't pay attention to the call after that because he was thinking about how strong the drug was, the dose from this morning seemingly making his headache resurface.

"Call me if you need anything." And the call ended there.

Sasha didn't want to stay in his room after that. For some reason, the thought of being indoors was beginning to irritate him and dampen his mood. Everything was too familiar and too close to his person. He realized the word he was searching for was *suffocating*. The room was suffocating. He took his largest umbrella and sliced his way into the still pouring rain. He thought about things he needed to restock in his fridge, trying his best not to focus on just one thing. He saw a group of children holding hands, covered only by raincoats, being led through the downpour by two women at the front. He realized they were holding on to a long rope with large plastic handles for their hands.

He went to the diner after a few blocks, his shoes now soaked through. He wasn't quite hungry yet, but he ordered the lunch special hamburger with Swiss and picked at the very hot, oily fries, eavesdropping on the conversation of the two waitresses, one of them talking about their classes at Kroft Technical for the first semester. That girl was interesting. Her name was Jamie. She had the brightest red hair he had ever seen and equally red eyebrows. Either it was real or it was a highly impressive dye job. Her eyes were a pale green. Her uniform was a pale blue skirt, white tucked-in shirt, and a black apron. Her shoes were short white canvas sneakers that had black laces. The laces looked newer.

He went back to the fries when the girl turned to look at him. He didn't like any of this. He didn't feel like himself. He didn't want the burger; what he wanted was a fatty piece of meat drenched in sauce. He continued eating it, though, feeling the flaky salt melt on his tongue. It seemed to help his headache.

Jamie walked over as he was focusing on eating, putting the tablet with his check on it in front of him. "No rush," Jamie said as she walked away and back around the main counter, starting to clean it of cups and plates.

He paid and left, not wanting to be seen as a creep. The rain had stopped, and the sun was beginning to appear at the end of the city square, falling on the hooves of the Maykis statue. The soot from before was now gone. It looked cleaner. The bronze base looked as though it had been shined.

His thoughts began to float to that day at the foot of the statue, the sizzling and crackle of the dolls burning in large groups. He could feel cold air on him at the moment, and though it wasn't used that day, the memories were starting to converge into one. He still had ringing in his ears from the protest before it. It was in these thoughts that he started to realize that Muse and Zora were really gone and that he would, if his dad could help it, never see them again.

He walked around the park with these thoughts, circling the mountain statue a few times before beginning to walk back to his apartment. He let his thoughts repeat about Muse, finding that with each go around, he could almost see her and feel her presence. He could feel the tightly woven thread run over the tips of his fingers, though he only touched her hair once in his life.

Back in his apartment, the light seemed to be tinged with the mint green skirt Muse would wear. Her voice, though, was the hardest to not focus on. He thought over and over again about the shocked whisper that fell from her lips when he kissed her. Each time in his mind's eye, he tried to hear it. He thought one time he heard the word *how*, but he stopped, knowing that wasn't true, and he really didn't hear anything. The memory was completely fabricated.

It was beginning to get dark when he thought to stop himself. When he took inventory, he realized he had ordered food at one point, though he didn't remember, and it was sitting on the counter next to the sink, which meant he went downstairs to get it, and he didn't remember that either. On the counter next to the files that his dad sent him over the months was the pill bottle. He took and poured the contents into the sink and turned on the garbage disposal. He swiped the lid off the counter of the sink into the garbage and turned on the disposal one more time to make sure it was all gone.

His food was already cold, but he continued to eat it. His fridge was close to empty, and he didn't think he'd have the mental fortitude to focus on the task of cooking without staring down a spatula for an hour. He hoped by the morning that the headache and the nauseating act of focusing for so long would be gone. His dad didn't tell him much about the drug, and he was afraid to start internet searches on it in the high chance he would find himself on the computer for hours and hours, just falling into hole after hole.

Rose Water

Amethyst

Amethyst was thankful not having to get into a car and actually stretch her limbs. She had felt so contained for a while. They walked down a long dirt road, passing by another similarly designed cottage on the right and a gas station with only one pump. Zircon and Judy were up ahead, saying nothing to each other but exchanging glances every so often.

At the end of a grassy field, Amethyst could see a little lake, gated and surrounded by signs stating that it was a protected site and not to cross the gate. She walked faster then, catching up with them in a few moments. They walked farther around the gate until they came on an area that was covered with overgrown leaves woven inside the chain link and somewhat rusted over at the poles. Zircon pulled on the right side of one of the panels, and it fell to the left side and dangled, revealing a curtain-like opening. They walked around the inside of this fence for a little while longer until they came on a large pebbly bank partially covered in moss.

There were another guy there and a woman with the same color of eyes who, Amethyst assumed, was his mother. The water smelled like perfume, especially with the sun beating down on the surface of the water and the top of her head. In that next moment, she saw the woman lead the guy into the water. The woman looked much younger than Judy. In her hand, she held flowers with long, woody stems. One was a creamy white color, the others purple. She spread these flowers around him, and they partially sank but still rose a bit on the surface of the water around them. She held her hands together in what looked like a prayer. She told him something that Amethyst could not discern, and he knelt in the water before he began to lower his face into the lake. He stayed this way for a while, the bubbles from his nose floating to the top before he suddenly jerked his body up like the water burned, but this was soon followed by a deep sigh. The woman wrapped her hands around him as he stayed kneeling.

Judy stood closer to her and held her shoulders similarly. "I want you to kneel like he is kneeling. Keep your head under the water until you hear the voice."

"Voice?"

The guy looked at her then and smiled with a goofy grin from ear to ear, letting his fingers trail along inside the water. Judy rubbed her back, and Amethyst couldn't help but jump at the touch. "Sorry . . . sorry. Take your time, OK?" Judy sounded like she had burned Amethyst and not just touched her back.

Amethyst looked down at the water; she could see swimming around small white fish and water striders on the surface. With each move of the water, she could see the deep, muddy green color of algae swaying back and forth, some of it being migrated to the bank. Amethyst scanned around the lake, noting its kidney bean shape and the patches of grass, sand, and pebbles that alternated all around the edge. She didn't look forward to knowing just how cold the water was, and although it was hot, the wind rattled the leaves on the fence. She turned and saw Zircon standing far behind, her hands folded in front of her at her waist. The look on her face was serious. Judy, on the other hand, was utterly serene.

Amethyst began kneeling but tripped a bit forward, wetting herself from the waist up. Her hands landed into the wet silt. She leaned forward; the water began to take on a weird appearance. She turned her head, seeing the guy and his mom begin walking away, her vision seeming clear and fine. When she looked back, the foggy quality returned, the smell even stronger from that distance. She thought maybe there must be something wrong with it—pollution. Nothing about the water felt strange. It didn't feel murky or thick; it was nice and cool. It only smelled like a bouquet buried in her nose. *Rose water* was the word. It smelled like rose water.

Amethyst got closer and let her hair fall into the water before she put her head under. It was refreshing. As she got deeper, she was beginning to feel odd, not sick but woozy. She listened, and all she could hear was the floating of bubbles to the surface. She was about to come up when the water suddenly felt warm; in a moment, it was hot, and softly she heard a male voice but could not make out the words. It sounded like Sasha. She pulled herself up, but there was resistance in the action, the burning feeling on her cheeks still there. She gasped, and deep in her chest, she felt her heart pound as if it was pressing into her rib cage.

Judy helped her stand up, the water sloshing around, mud covering her jeans. "Come, let's get you dry. You've done a good job. I know it's a bit scary, but there's nothing else you need to do. It's done." She sounded sad. She said the words *it's done,* and Amethyst could not help but notice this. Anyone would have heard the sadness in her voice.

Zircon walked ahead, almost like she couldn't get away fast enough, her shoes pounding into the soft dirt with every forceful yet measured step. When they caught up with Zircon, she didn't pay mind to Amethyst.

They walked back, and Judy drew a bath for her. In the bath, Amethyst soaked herself, expecting the burning feeling to return to her face. She wet her face, patted it, and rubbed her hands over it, letting the soap build up a foam, but there was no burning sensation; and if she was honest, she was probably on her way to cause her own kind of rash if she kept soaping and drying out her face. She didn't feel any different on the inside than yesterday.

Her rash was gone, which was the only thing causing her to feel a level of trust. Their green remedy worked. The only thing she could do for now was to wait for the next bout of pain to appear. Four months—that felt like a fair amount of time. She came out and dried herself in front of the mirror, looking at her face the whole time, expecting something to be revealed in the mirror in the new light but nothing.

When she came into the room adjoining the bathroom, there was a new white gauzy top and a pair of light-colored blue jeans folded on the bed. Next to it was a small black box with a blue ribbon. She dressed; the pants were a little big around the waist but fit everywhere else, and the top fit perfectly. She held the box in her hands for a moment, debating with herself if she wanted to accept it. She guessed it was jewelry. Amethyst walked down the stairs with it, smelling something cooking downstairs.

Judy was sitting on the couch, listening to music, and Zircon was in the kitchen, cooking. The living room was warm and smelled peppery.

"Come, let me put it on you," Judy said, getting up from the couch.

She wore a long green dress, changing out of the pants and T-shirt she wore this morning.

"You didn't have to get me anything. Really, it's OK," Amethyst said.

It immediately solicited a confused look from Judy. "It's your mask. You're required to wear it until you're of majority age." She walked closer. "I know that masks have become more of an official thing in the Bluebird Territory, only graduations, on Presidents', but here, we usually wear them in our everyday life . . . like watches." Judy placed her hand on the box. "You don't have to wear it now, but it's expected while you're out in public spaces. I thought I would show you around Diamond Sea."

"Oh, oh, OK." Amethyst nodded. Carefully, Amethyst removed the ribbon and opened the box; the mask was folded over a piece of cream-colored cardstock. The bridge, where the clasp at the edge and the right side met, had a light blue stripe on it, indicating Bluebird citizenship.

Judy said solemnly, "It's not official, of course, but I didn't want to erase the fact you lived there and had a life there." She smiled. "A lot of moms, like me, are doing the same. Maybe you'll find some of your friends." Judy nodded, more to herself, it seemed, as her head was bowed.

Amethyst didn't say a word as she removed the mask from the box, feeling the silk at the edge's side across her fingertips. The ribbon tail was long, not yet cut to form to her face. The last time she wore her Bluebird Territory mask was at high school graduation. And after that, nothing. She didn't even remember how to adjust the straps anymore or if it was a different method. "Can you—"

"Yes, absolutely." Judy unraveled the mask from the box and stood behind Amethyst. She took a comb out and began making a part separating the back of her hair from the crown. "Hold," Judy said as she held up the crown portion of her hair.

Amethyst held it up, and Judy put the mask on her face, adjusting the clasp and tying in right in the middle of the part. "Thank you," Amethyst said as she turned around.

"You want me to trim the tails?"

"No, it's OK." Amethyst didn't mind them; her hair was now halfway down her back, and it completely concealed them in her dark hair. Amethyst fought back the tears that were forming in her eyes, blinking them back, but this exercise didn't help. Her tears came, getting caught in the fabric of the mask.

"Let's eat. She should be almost done. I made some buns," Judy said as she led Amethyst to the kitchen.

Diamond Sea

Amethyst

The city center of Diamond Sea was a concentrated block of shops and skyscrapers that dwarfed the modest houses in the distance. It formed a circle, and if it wasn't for the small trails of sand on the sidewalk, you wouldn't know that just behind the tightly packed buildings was a beachfront town. It was a clearly planned city, separated into four quadrants on a grid system. It creeped Amethyst out how easy it was for her to figure out where everything was in the first try. They walked along the innermost streets, around the statue of Pres. Luke Talis, circling around the shops that were each part of a large circular building. Everyone was well dressed; pretty much everyone wore a mask, which made telling people apart difficult. Amethyst stayed close to Judy.

"I want to stop here. You guys don't have to wait for me." Zircon went inside a stationery shop and left the pair.

Judy turned toward Amethyst. "This store is famous. You want to go in?"

"No, that's all right." She wondered if her phone had enough charge to even work for payment.

"My treat."

"I just need a phone charger."

"Ah, come with me. We'll go to Digits."

Digits was just on the opposite side of the inner circle. It was a tech store with a long, winding staircase, keeping in spirit with the rest of the architecture. Amethyst went over to the communicators display, looking at each of them, trying to find her own. They didn't have the same model on display as hers. She was two models behind.

"Help?" a tall man asked her, placing his hands on the display stand. Amethyst couldn't help but to notice the onyx ring on his ring finger.

"Yeah, I need a charger for this communicator." Amethyst held it up.

"We have the charger, but you might need another connector so it will fit in the outlet. That phone is exclusive to the Bluebird Territory—ah, I see, you're from there." He pointed to the area on his mask where the bit of blue was on her own.

He walked her toward a wall for universal chargers and handed her the connector she would need. Amethyst triple-checked the charger box to make sure it charged her phone, and he allowed her to take the charger and connector out and test it in one of their outlets. It fit. Judy bought it for her, and they headed toward the front door.

On their way out, she saw something that would have helped in the first place, a large poster showing all the Bluebird communicators and their appropriate charger compatibility with Crow Territory communicators. Standing next to it was a guy with the same blue strip as her. He had the same shade of blond hair as Sasha, but his was long. There was no way that he could have grown his hair that fast.

"They're against that wall," Amethyst said.

"Thanks. Do you have this one?" He took out his communicator; it was the same model as Amethyst's.

"Same one. It's charger type B and an outlet connector."

"I appreciate this. My phone's been dead for a solid two days."

They went their separate ways, and Amethyst and Judy left Digits. And all she could think about was just how long her phone had been dead. They took the train back whose path was right dead center in the circle and ran every thirty minutes from the circle and to the seaside town. The walk from the train wasn't a long one, and once home, all Amethyst could think about was charging her phone and calling her mom. Judy, seemingly all knowing, gave Amethyst her space.

Amethyst pulled the phone in the bathroom outlet and waited for the charge to go from critical to low before opening her messages. There was only one. "They're not going to charge us. Judy didn't want to press charges for kidnapping. Can you fucking believe that? Kidnapping?"

Amethyst called her mom immediately. It took her a few moments to pick up. She had to try the call twice. "Hello?"

"Amie."

"Are you OK?"

"No. Are you OK?"

"I'm fine. It's just great to hear your voice. I would have called you, but my phone doesn't work without a special charger, and . . . they've been helping me with my pain. I can't really explain much of it. I don't really know what's going on, but I'm fine . . . don't cry . . . I'm fine. I just don't want you guys to go to jail or anything." Amethyst let the words flow from her mouth.

"We're OK. Josh went to see Lucy about helping another family. They only questioned me."

"Wait, why?"

"I don't know, Amie. How are you eating over there?"

"I don't understand why they wouldn't question him. He had fake documents too. And he was in the car, not that I want anything to happen to him, but it doesn't make sense."

"It doesn't make sense, but I'm not gonna go to the Authority and say, 'Hey, you forgot to arrest my friend.' Amethyst, they're only concerned with the adoptive parents. I've been on the boards, and other parents who lost their kids are saying the same thing, that they just arbitrarily punish parents if they run. Some people get off scot-free, but some are taken to jail for a few months. I don't get them. It's not like we're hurting you."

Amethyst didn't know how to respond because she knew it wasn't that simple. The rash she had on her face was only fixed here. Her mom didn't know what to do with her, and indirectly, she was being hurt by her lack of knowledge. "Have you spoken to Muse, Sasha, or Zora?"

"I'm sorry, Amie. Muse was arrested a few days ago. Zora was as well. They were involved in an attempted bombing at Hunter's Point Mall. They're in the Crow Territory. I don't know where. I'm guessing jail, but none of the news channels are talking about what they're gonna do with them. Sasha's still here, but I haven't talked to him in a while. I saw him at the café a day ago, but I couldn't get his attention."

"Why would they do that?" Amethyst nearly yelled; she didn't understand any of it.

"I'm 100 percent sure it was Muse. She started a fire in the square. She's not someone you want to involve yourself with. Her mother isn't even talking about her."

"How is that OK?"

"Honey, she might be embarrassed. Muse was arrested right in the middle of the park in front of her. There were TerraTech officials there and everything."

"But like everyone is doing stuff that's illegal at worst and questionable at best." Amethyst couldn't contain her annoyance or anger.

"How's the rash?"

"It's gone. It just went away on its own." Amethyst didn't feel like explaining anything now. She already had a lot she wanted to go over in her head. She didn't have the energy to tell her mom what happened in the pond.

"Good, Amie. Maybe it was just an allergic reaction. I'm glad you're OK. Call me more often, OK?

"OK." And with that, her mom hung up.

Amethyst immediately began trying Sasha's number. She couldn't stand to be left out of the loop like she had been. The first time he didn't pick up, and the second time he did. It took a while to connect; she supposed he had another call, and once it did, Sasha sounded so groggy. "I knew you'd come back to me."

Amethyst didn't like how he said that. "Hey, Sasha."

"How have you been? Are you on a beach somewhere?"

"I am. How are you?"

"Honestly, by a thread, but it's nice to hear your voice."

"You sound really tired."

"Well, it's not exactly a secret that some quote, unquote 'children' are changing. And because of this, my dad thought it would be a good idea to try to suppress this with Cerplex. I had no idea if it even works, but pfft! What could it hurt? I didn't take it this morning though. It made me feel weird."

"Because it's a compliance drug, Sasha! Why would your dad think that works?"

"He's done his research. I don't know. All I know is I'm never taking it again."

"I can't get unstuck from the idea he gave you that. I'm sorry. I'll stop.

You can't change that man, but, Sasha, you do know that drug stays in your system for, like, days. Maddy was on it because she got caught running away too many times." Amethyst remembered how odd her cousin became; she would stare off into space and obsess over wax dripping down from the candles on the kitchen table, regardless if it was lit or not.

"Once he's doing something, he finishes it. You know that."

"Oh, yeah, I know that."

"Don't sound so surprised. You're smarter than that. We both know he's a—"

"Monster," Amethyst finished.

"Why did you call me?" He sounded annoyed.

"Because Muse and Zora were arrested. They tried to burn a building down—I mean, tried to bomb it and burn down the square."

"No, Muse tried to burn down the square, and Zora and Muse tried to bomb a mall. And yes, those two things happened. I couldn't stop them. They were set in their paths before I knew what was going on. If I could go back in time, I would have stopped them. I'm not OK with arson."

"How is everything, besides all that?"

"Shit."

"Oh."

"All of you guys are just scattered in the wind, and I'm here literally watching raindrops. It's a steaming pile."

"Do you have any idea where they are?"

"No. He doesn't trust me. And even if I did, I wouldn't be able to do anything. They're good as gone."

"I mean, could they be in the Crow Territory?"

"Most likely. They lost their rights protesting. They didn't get trials. Why would that matter though? Aren't you on the run?"

"I am, but I just want to know if they're OK."

"I'm sorry, Amie. I don't know. I'm gonna go back to bed, OK?"

"OK."

He hung up after a moment, and once the line went dead, Amethyst could not help but let her tears flow. It felt like she was punched in the gut. Sasha was not himself. Every trace of light he once was seemed to be zapped right out of him, and Muse and Zora were as he said it, "scattered in the wind." And here she was, scared to tell anyone what was really happening, in the bathroom, afraid to do anything in public out of fear of her "new" mom. Judy didn't seem to mind her calling other people, but it would be ridiculous to think that, to any degree, it was the truth.

This new place she couldn't explain to other people. How was she supposed to tell anyone about a magic pond that cured her of all her ailments? It was too odd that they didn't have to worry about her telling anyone because who would believe her? She leaned over the sink and ran some cold water on her hands and wet her face, dampening the mask further. It was nice to know that the mask could hide her tears.

There was a knock at the door, and then came Judy's voice. "Is everything OK in there? Is there anything I can do?"

"I'm fine. I'm coming out now," Amethyst said as she unplugged the phone and walked toward the door. When she opened it, she saw Judy holding a little white poodle.

"We have guest. There are some people I want you to meet," Judy said as she raked her hand along the side of the poodle's curly fur.

Guest

Amethyst

Folding chairs were pulled out for the overflow of guests who were in Zircon's living room. There were five people, not counting them. Judy sat with Zircon on the couch, and Amethyst sat next to a tall, long-haired blond woman who kept her legs nicely folded the entire time. Three men sat together on the opposite end of the couch. Each of them had small paper plates of crackers and cheese balanced on their knees. Someone had brought a tray of cookies in shapes and flavors Amethyst had never seen before. Some of them looked like rosebuds and others like seashells. On the table was a pile of journals wrapped in a thick white ribbon. Amethyst watched the conversation unfold in front of her, still repeating in her head everything that Sasha had said to her.

It began with the weather and soon migrated to the kitchen around a couple of bottles of wine where they, as a group, remembered their time in high school together. "I remember that test, five questions, and all of them took three pages to answer. I was ready to walk out of the building and sell ribbons on the street corner."

Amethyst didn't understand what Judy meant by this apart from they were students at the same time, and this didn't make sense to her because Judy looked much older than the rest of them.

"Selling ribbons on the street corner doesn't mean what you think it does," Zircon whispered into Amethyst's ear.

"What does it mean?"

"Um, nightwalkers."

"Oh, OK." And now she was only more confused because what did ribbons have to do with any of that?

Judy offered Amethyst some wine, but she refused, wanting to pay close attention to the conversation. She was learning so much that she didn't want to miss anything by being buzzed.

"Mr. Davis is still there. My daughter had him for her senior capstone. He's still the same hard ass as he was before," Drew said.

"I mean, if he just knew that twelve-year-olds weren't ready to write dissertations, he'd be all right." Judy laughed.

"True," Drew said, raising his glass as if to toast.

"Have you thought of your arrangements?" the tall woman, who was quiet most of the night, said. She had drunk more wine than anyone else, finishing a bottle on her own. She didn't appear drunk, but she was careful when she walked around the kitchen island in her heels.

"Let's not talk about that now," Judy said back firmly, making a cursory glance at Amethyst. "I want to show you something." She put down her glass a little hard. She took Amethyst back into the living room and placed the stack of books into her arms. "It's my journals from my childhood up until now. I thought it would be easier to tell you where I've been and what I've done through my journals. I know it is hard to be plopped here and not really explained much of anything. So please take them." Judy nodded yes and placed her hand on top of the books. "It would mean a lot to me if you took them. You don't have to read them now, but if you're ever curious, they're there."

"Thank you." Amethyst couldn't say no to this. It was too big of a thing to say no to. The house was filled with unfamiliar people, and slowly, they emerged from the kitchen and watched them. Zircon's eyes were glassy as she watched and slightly red from drinking.

"I think I'm gonna go to bed, if that's OK." But the truth was she wanted to go to her room and call Sasha back. She didn't like how the last call ended.

"Yes. I'll bring you some fresh towels. Get some rest," Judy said, her eyes trailing over Amethyst's face.

Amethyst took the journals upstairs and placed them on the nightstand beside her bed. The ribbon was crumpled from her holding it against her chest. She knew she shouldn't feel so odd about the journals; Judy was her biological mom, but it all felt too personal too fast. The mask she was OK with. It was a far practical gift. The charger was OK too. A week hadn't even passed before she was given all of her biological mother's secrets.

She went to the bathroom for her phone and found Zircon sitting on her bed when she got back. "Mom gave you a great gift, and you should think carefully about how you treat it and her. It's not easy for anyone to have their kid stolen and have to fight to get them back." Her voice was threatening.

"I didn't say I didn't want it."

"Oh my god, Amethyst. Open your eyes a little bit. Has nothing changed since your time at the lake?" Zircon said as she stood, her hands migrating to her hips.

"My face doesn't burn, and that's more or less it."

Can you hear this?

Amethyst nodded, her feet feeling like she was on uneven ground. Her heart felt as if it shifted in her chest, sitting uncomfortably on her lungs.

I can hear you and what you're saying inside your head, and you've been just ungrateful half the time. She's mom, not biological mom. You know you're adopted. Why are you making this so hard?

"I'm sorry." Amethyst walked back to the bathroom and closed the door.

I'm not feeding into your sulking. Be careful with Sasha. You can't trust that family. They are part of the reason the famine happened in the first place. Yeah, Sasha's dad had a hand in it.

"Sasha hates his dad," Amethyst said softly.

"No . . . no, he doesn't. Upset maybe, but he doesn't hate him quite yet. He let his dad rake Muse through the mud and did nothing about it. That boy is truly lost. And what Sasha feels about his dad doesn't mean that he doesn't condone what he does."

"I thought you wanted me to just accept that I was adopted, but you're OK with the protesters?"

"I think they have spunk. I don't blame them. I don't blame you either, but there's a certain level of respect you have to give to Mom. If these protesting kids don't get help, more of them are going to die, or their transformations are going to continue to stall. Have you been paying attention to what has been happening tonight?"

"No, I really don't understand. Please just tell me." Amethyst couldn't help her tone.

"Mom is literally aging because your transformation was continually stalled. Older kids like Muse, Sasha, and Zora are doing the same thing to their parents but to a higher degree. If we had not gotten you here, you would have died, and Mom would have been stuck alive."

"What do you mean stuck alive?"

"We need you here so Mom can die. Crows can't die without the youngest child transforming. If that child dies before the parent, then the parent doesn't die, and the family line is broken. You're the youngest, so you're the only one who can have children."

"That doesn't make any sense whatsoever."

"Even if you don't believe me, it's still true. You know as well as I do that Crow children were dropping like flies, and no one could figure it out." Zircon sat back on the bed. "Just come out of the bathroom, please, so I can see your face," Zircon called out to her.

Amethyst emerged, tears streaking her face.

"It's not common knowledge because it's a closely guarded secret, and you can't tell Sasha this, even though he should know because we can't trust what his family would do with that kind of information. OK?"

"OK."

"I thought you would've caught on that Mom looks older than all her high school friends. You're not that old, Amethyst. I'm not. Why would Mom be?"

"So we just let Sasha's dad drug him?"

"Sasha's gene is most likely dormant at this point. He's nearly twenty-one. He's not going to die. And neither will his parents."

"Where's our dad?"

"He left us. He's still alive though." Zircon sounded sad as she spoke.

"Will he die too?"

"Yes, and he knows this."

The conversation fizzled out at that point. Amethyst didn't know what else to say, and Zircon turned the conversation back to the party, so Amethyst washed her face with cool water and went back to the gathering occurring downstairs.

"But you wouldn't know looking at her she was the best tennis player in our grade."

"I only had two games more than my classmates. It wasn't by much . . . if you add—

"She's modest."

Judy was sitting on the couch as Drew stood by the mantel, making serving motions. Once Judy saw Amethyst, she motioned her over, making room between herself and the woman who wasn't speaking. Amethyst heard more stories that night, and it continued like this until they left, all going their separate ways. Zircon stood near the wall the whole night, watching Amethyst. As they cleaned for the night, Zircon sat on the patio, finishing a dry red wine and cookies.

"Judy," Amethyst began as she swept crumbs into her hand from the coffee table, "what do ribbons have to do with being . . . paid company?"

"Well, here, some of them sell things as a kind of lure for men. Could be handkerchiefs, hair ribbons, flowers. That was when I was a girl though. It's mostly on the internet now," Judy said.

"I see."

"Before you go to bed, I want to clarify some things for you. I heard you and Zircon talking upstairs, and first of all, I'm not upset with you, OK? I'm not. I don't blame you for feeling like you do. I just want to know I left you with as much of me as possible so you don't regret anything." Judy said this while standing in the kitchen threshold.

Amethyst could hear Zircon groan from the patio.

"Ignore her. She's been like this for three years now." Judy laughed, and Amethyst didn't understand what was humorous. She was dying, and it was because of her.

It would have been stupid that Amethyst thought to ask her what the time frame was of her dying, and so internally, she tried to bury that thought so Zircon couldn't get to it.

"I can hear some of what is on your mind, and the answer is it will depend on how soon you develop your gift."

"But I can already hear—"

"Then it won't be long off. This has been happening for hundreds of years. It's not new to us." Judy walked closer. "I've been expecting this since you were sixteen. I'm ready for this."

A tight feeling was beginning in Amethyst's chest, and her eyes stung in the anticipation of tears. Her entire body felt light, like it was floating.

"I'll get you some water," Judy said quickly as she walked over to the sink.

Amethyst was on the floor, sitting at the foot of the bed, when she came back. The tightness of her chest was restricting the space she had to breathe.

"Let's not talk about it. I think we've made much of the last few days about me that it would, for me at least, be nice to know about you. A lot has happened." Judy spoke slowly.

"Yeah, yes, a lot." Amethyst didn't speak for a moment after that, absorbing all that was happening in the room.

"So how clearly can you hear?" Judy sounded really excited, crossing her legs and leaning forward.

Amethyst sat up. "I can hear it like I can hear you talking to me right now but not all the time."

"Zircon is talented at keeping her thoughts down, so to speak. They're there. When you focus, you might hear them. There's a lot of noise out there interrupting."

"Do you listen?"

"I try not to. I try to give her some privacy."

"So everyone can hear?" Amethyst wondered just how much people knew about her from her thoughts.

"No, it's only people from our line who still can. It's a dying-out gift." Judy sounded sad as she spoke.

"How many can?"

"Besides us, including my ex-husband, only one other, but he'd be your half brother."

"Will I meet him?"

"I have no idea where the kid is. I just know of him. I tried my best to keep my distance from that toxic chapter of my life. He would be a little older than you are. He was adopted out as well. That is as far as I know. I don't know his name. I didn't want to know about the other woman." Judy spoke toward her interlaced fingers.

"A lot of people in my class year were adopted as well. The school is famous for having the highest numbers. I've been reading the forums, and there's supposed to be a demonstration there tomorrow."

"We're you involved in all that?"

"No, my adoptive mom didn't let me. She said it was too dangerous to attract that kind of attention. Some of my friends did. They even led some. Muse set the Maykis statue on fire."

Judy laughed at this and abruptly covered her mouth, catching herself. "I don't like the Maykises either," she said between suppressed giggles. She looked like a girl as she laughed.

"What did they do?"

"They Maykises are in the pocket of TerraTech. They've been using silver flower, and it only grows here, so they bought up a lot of our land to harvest it. We have very little of it left to use for healing, but they have plenty of it to use for experiments or whatever the hell they're using it for. I don't know how useful it's gonna be for them seeing as they don't know what we have been using it for. It's a mess, really messy exactly. I should not sugarcoat it. Even Zircon, who has been in the kitchen with me, making medicines, has difficulty. I have faith in her though. She'll get it perfectly one day." Judy spoke so fast that it was hard for Amethyst to keep up; she was still stuck on the laugh about the Maykis statue.

She wasn't expecting that reaction. Zircon more or less condemned what they were doing on the basis that they were sick and needed help, but Judy, on the other hand, looked gleeful at the thought of a statue going up in flames. They were very different people.

"TerraTech may be a Crow company, but it doesn't look out for Crow interest. No one does anything because they made it so we need them for pretty much everything." Judy readjusted her sitting posture and took a deep breath.

"I don't like them. They're everywhere in the Bluebird Territory. They set up security everywhere that is triggered when a protest gets too loud or even if there's a big crowd. They don't want anything said about them. You get emails even if you search the name TerraTech too much because they can't really tell your intentions."

"That's just a scare tactic. They tried to do it here too, but Pres. Luke Talis wouldn't allow it. He said he would rather spend the money modernizing the roads, and as you can see, he didn't really do that. All the money went into that high-tech city center." Judy nodded, her lips going into a tight line.

"They've been using tear gas. I think it's gone beyond just trying to scare people." Amethyst tried to put it as lightly as she could.

"I agree with you, Amethyst." Judy sounded offended. Her eyes were wide.

"I'm sorry. Um, can we talk about something else?" Amethyst began to stand up, trying to put some distance between her and the situation that was beginning. She didn't want to be thought of an ungrateful person. Zircon already thought she was, and she didn't want to just confirm that by obsessing over what was happening in the Bluebird Territory and how bad things had happened there. She couldn't win with this line of conversation.

Judy stood as well, her posture regal and light, and seemed to be thinking carefully about the next thing she was going to say. She started a sentence but stopped herself and then after a moment said, "I want you to feel like you can be yourself here. The only thing I want to know is what you really think. I want to get to know you as much as I can before I go. Don't sugarcoat anything for me. I don't get how you feel because I can't imagine what it must be like. I want to know as much of your story as I can," Judy finished.

Amethyst felt the all-too-familiar sting in her eyes in that moment, watching Judy stand, somewhat unsteadily now, watching the traces of an apology on her face.

Cards

Amethyst

Amethyst woke up the next day to the sound of the rain and thunder that jostled her out of her deep, heady sleep. A strong urge to go downstairs was there in the pit of her stomach. She remembered everything that night so clearly, like every thought was said two times over. Amethyst didn't know what she wanted to say or even what was appropriate to say, but she was sure she needed to be there with Judy.

Downstairs, Judy was sitting on the patio. Zircon was beside her as they opened cards. "Come help us," Judy said over her shoulder.

Spread about the table were colorful cards, some decorated with rosebuds, others with blooming flowers, some with intricate line designs that formed square-shaped mountain peaks. In a box were even more unopened cards.

"These are from family. The other stack is from friends. The less pretty ones are from banks, restaurants. I went to a lot . . . I'm gonna need an album or something," Judy said softly.

"I'll buy you one," Zircon said, taking out another piece of cardstock and starting to write.

"Want to help open cards? You can keep any money you find." Judy turned around and smiled.

Amethyst sat at the table and took out a card from the box. It was powder blue, which was her favorite color. The card in soft blues lined with a darker blue read, "Always in my thoughts."

"That's a little heavy, and I also highly doubt that." Judy laughed.

These were condolence cards, and the thought hit her so hard that she had to blink. "My close friends know to send the funny ones, maybe an insult, but the ones who are still touchy send the sappy ones." Judy took the card from Amethyst. "Look, she only signed it, no message."

This was the craziest thing that Amethyst had ever witnessed. She was dying and reading her own condolence cards, and she wasn't certain, but she was sure the party she attended last night was a funeral for all intents and purposes. "Is there a way to know?" Amethyst couldn't contain it anymore.

"I don't feel any different, but then again, I'm not sick. I'm just going to die. Rebecca took about a week before her daughter's transformation before the process began." She paused for a moment. "It looks a lot like the flu."

Amethyst continued the process of opening cards for Zircon to write thank-you cards for, putting any money she found to the side. She didn't want to talk anymore, and the repetitive, simple task was the most peace she had felt in ages. The rain smelled lovely on the patio, and the sound of drops hitting the rafters was like a natural metronome. There wasn't anything she could do to stop what was happening, but she could easily do this. She could open cards, she could read them, she could take the money out and stack it perfectly.

In the quiet rhythm of this, it wasn't easy to keep her mind focused on the task. Her mind strayed to the conversation from last night. Judy wanted to know what her story was, and Amethyst didn't know how to begin a task like that. Her story was wrapped up so much in what was happening that it was hard to detach from it. The last two years of her life were trying to tightly hold on to being a Bluebird, while strangers told her she was not. Her old life now seemed like a faded backdrop, whereas everything else was in true Technicolor. Much of it, by what had happened, was just a temporary rest stop to where she ended up. It was easier not to speak about it, easier to tuck it away into a box.

Zircon didn't seem to like her mentioning Sasha or his family, but the whole truth of it was Sasha's dad watched her as a child, came to her birthday parties, and came to her lacrosse games. And what was she to make of what Zircon said? If he was truly a monster, he wore a good mask.

Jump Start

Sasha

The gears in Sasha's mind turned slowly in the immediate moments after the phone call, but once they screeched to life, he experienced every moment of Amethyst on the phone with him in slow motion. He knew what he had done by talking to her, but he could not help picking up the phone. He wanted to hear her voice. He wanted to reach over to the side she was on, one that was uncomplicated and not wrapped up with the Authority and TerraTech and protesters.

The cell phone was still in his hand when he went to the bathroom, and he sat there fully clothed, holding it. He didn't remember why he went in there in the first place. When he left the bathroom, he realized he had to go but chose instead to drink more water. He was trying somewhat unsuccessfully to flush his system of the drug. After another twenty ounces, he would go to the bathroom and attempt to go to bed. It was nearly midnight. He still could not help focusing on things. He saw a spiderweb in the window and counted the little rungs on the web over and over again until his eyes hurt from the process.

His dad had called earlier, but he left a voice mail only stating that he needed to send along a log of when he was taking the medication. He repeated himself so much that Sasha felt like he was reliving the same day over again.

"I have to get up," he said to himself, resisting the urge to count how many black tiles were outlining his shoes. He got up, thrusting himself forward to get his body in motion as fast as possible. The more he was still, the more likely he was to hyperfocus. It was an awful feeling. It was painful.

He left the bathroom and got his huge bottle of water and continued to chug. The phone was still in his hand. It took him a while now to recalibrate what his body was doing. He put it down and focused just on drinking, a hard lump of water going down his throat.

He sat on the couch then and turned on the TV. The first thing that showed up was a cartoon, not one he watched. It was something new for kids now. It was weird, mostly blue tinged. It was a welcome distraction. Tomorrow was the protest, and he thought about not going. He hadn't been in the building in such a long time that it would be weird to be back there. He was nearly twenty-one. The auditorium was also his least favorite place after the announcement. Sasha had never felt such anger before then. In the time before the announcement, it was his favorite place.

Sasha got up from the couch and turned off the TV, finding having it on and thinking too difficult to do at the same time. Everything seemed so loud. He dialed his dad, hoping for it to go to voice mail so he could say he'd be sending a long log and should be left alone for a while, but after a split second, it connected, and he heard his dad saying hello over the sound of running water. The water was shut off, and his dad began talking somewhat slowly. "How are you feeling?"

"A little out of it. I don't really like this drug."

"Well, it's only for a few months. It's proven effective at suppressing the gene in that time frame."

Sasha couldn't imagine taking the drug for that long. He didn't even want to think about what it would do to his mind in that time frame. "Oh, ah, I thought about going to the protest in the gym. Want to get back into it." The truth was he didn't want to get back into anything. He just wanted to get off the subject of the drug.

"Oh, you don't have to worry about that anymore. We think we triangulated where Amethyst is. How about helping with that instead?"

"Amethyst is not hurting anyone. Why do you need her now?" He knew she would be changing soon, but it clearly didn't happen yet by the way she sounded. His dad didn't need to get involved. He could just give her the drug his dad had given him the first time he was about to transform. There was no reason to drag her back.

"She's your closest friend, and I want to help her. I know her mom must be concerned about her. She returned without her."

"What do you mean?"

"It appears that Arnett just merely dropped Amethyst off. I don't know where. Do you know where?"

"I don't. She didn't say."

"Are you sure you don't know or you don't want to tell me? I can find her. I thought you might want to make is easier for me."

"Nope."

"Sasha."

"I think you should just leave her be. She only ran. Are you gonna now arrest kids who run?"

"Are you really asking me if I'm gonna risk a family friend dying?"

"Amethyst is *my* friend." And with that, Sasha hung up the phone.

TURPEEK II

Marcus

Marcus tried to call back, but it went straight to voice mail. He hoped Sasha would take the bait and just tell him himself. It would make it easier in the long run. If Sasha felt it was his fault, he'd blame himself for everything that happened thereafter, and Marcus wouldn't have to fix anything, only wait for some time to pass. He knew where she was, but he didn't know the situation. He was still waiting for information from the Authority.

Marcus was in the middle of getting ready to look at the documents for the experiment. He hoped it was working, but if he was honest with himself, it was too early to know whether it worked on most. The document was sealed like a present on his kitchen island, ready to be opened. He got a glass of wine and reheated leftover fried rice and began opening.

The top cases were those who were Sasha's age, and it showed a trend he was not expecting. Over the last few days, the vital signs for those Sasha's age had been decreasing below normal rates. It was a sharp decrease. He paged through the file to find any specifics and found a line with Muse's specific numbers, and even hers had been decreasing at the same rate despite her just starting. It was like they were responding to something in unison.

Marcus closed the file but soon reopened it, wondering if those who were younger were experiencing the same trend. It wasn't as drastic, but it was happening. The gene was suppressed in all of them, and the descent of their vitals happened between a couple of weeks, like Zora and Muse, and a couple of months.

He got up from the couch and walked to his room, the light dimmed to 30 percent. In the pale light, he began packing a bag. First he would go to the lab to get some supplies, and after that, he would head to the Crow Territory; if he started driving nonstop, he would be there in ten hours. He packed enough for a few days, still unsure of when the Authority would get back to him about her living situation.

On his way out, he powered down the apartment, the sound of weakening charges echoing down the halls. He walked to the covered lot at the back of the complex and climbed into the black SUV. The drive to the lab was quiet, not many people on the road at that hour. As he wove up the winding hill toward the campus, he saw the shiny glass ball come into view.

In his office, he grabbed some testing kits and sample mailers. Whichever lab got it first would be the one he would work with to isolate whatever gene Amethyst seemed to have. Back in the car, he sent an email explaining where he was going to his superiors before turning off his tracker on both his cell phone and car. It would be easier on Sasha if it was truly too difficult for him to help Amethyst. The guilt would be too much for him otherwise.

The suburb wasn't far from Moss Point; from there, he would get to Turpeek and finally Diamond Sea. He debated with himself as he started driving if he should tell Sasha what he knew about Amethyst. But he shook the thought out of his head. Sasha had no longer become dependable. Even if he explained that he wasn't going to harm Amethyst, Sasha would still be offended that he wanted to test on her. Sasha was manageable. He had been since he met Zora and Muse.

Am I in Danger?

Sasha

Sasha held the cell phone in his hand, trying to decide what was worth doing. He didn't think Amethyst would pick up, and honestly, he didn't blame her, and he didn't think begging with his dad to leave her alone would result in anything. But he knew he had to make a choice. His heart was pounding in his ears, and an all-too-familiar feeling was settling in his gut. It was the same feeling he had when he kissed Muse. It was a dark feeling. It was a gray cloud that slowly rolled in.

Despite it being nearly two in the morning, he had the most energy he had all day. He looked at the balance of his account, praying that it hadn't increased as his dad's way of saying, "Thank you for sacrificing your friend." It hadn't changed. It was still the same. But that really didn't mean anything. He hadn't received anything right away for Muse or Zora, and his dad suspecting his reaction cut off all his ability to track anything he was doing when he was going after Zora for her part in the bombing attempt at Hunter's Point. He couldn't trust his dad's inaction as indication he had discovered any decency.

Sasha decided to wash, get dressed, and just start driving north. His car, which he rarely used, was parked in the garage in the basement of the complex. Sasha took another look around the mess that was beginning again before heading to the bathroom. Maybe he would eat something other than pizza or reheated pizza tomorrow morning.

The shower was tepid and did not feel refreshing at all. He was impatient to put on clothes. The walk to the car felt longer than normal. He walked all the way down the hall toward stairway L, took a few flights down, and traversed another concrete hall before coming on the garage. He took his card out of his wallet to scan at the checkpoint, and he began to go down the winding exit. The checkpoint was empty, so he had to scan at the machine before the gates opened.

On the way out, he felt the brisk air cut through the open passenger window. The lights still had full strength as it was still very dark. It was 3:40 a.m. by the time he pulled into the street and began to go toward the highway headed toward Moss Point. He would call her in the morning to find out more about where she was located.

The road was empty, so each streetlight he came on was an even greater annoyance. He thought about what he would eat in the morning. He had spent so much energy stressing about what to do about Amethyst. Realizing what he was doing wrong, he turned off his tracker to his car and phone and texted Regina a lie that he was going to Clayton to clear his head. If he didn't give anyone a heads-up, that could send in their approval code; then it would be flagged as suspicious, and he could be tracked through other means. Regina replied at 5:13 a.m. and texted, "Yeah." It bought him some time. It might not be enough, but it was something. As the sun began to rise, more cars appeared in his rearview mirror, driving in the same direction. He wondered then how many of them were runners.

He didn't really think about what running might have been like for Amethyst. He had the protection of TerraTech that prevented his biological parents from doing anything. It also helped that he looked so much like his adoptive dad, and that must have been his intention. Sasha only felt adrenaline when he was protesting, and he could help that. In his everyday life, things were calm for the most part. The only times they weren't were when his dad wanted him to do something he wanted. Those times were the most stressful, but they usually passed. This was the only time in his life where it was constant.

He had to refocus a few times when he first started driving because he was speeding and gripping the steering wheel so hard, and he didn't notice, but the drug that was still swimming in his system helped him drive the best he ever had. His legs were getting tired from being at a constant angle. A little while longer, he turned into a park parking lot and got out.

It was filled with people watching a duck race on the pond, indicated by a large banner at the starting line. The starting line was decorated with big flowers shaped into a ball, attached to a long stick. The pair looked like lollipops. It seemed to be ending because the shouting and cheering was dying down to soft claps. Someone had won, but he couldn't tell from his distance. Most of the people he saw were just heads floating above the hill in front of them. Sasha watched until the crowd began to dissipate.

Back on the road, he plugged in information for a hotel and drove in that direction. He felt a little less foggy minded that afternoon in his hotel, and he wasn't sure if it was the drive or the lessening potency of Cerplex. When he woke up from his nap, he saw he had a texts from Amethyst.

"U OK?"

"Are you awake now?"

It was hours ago, and he didn't even notice them, which concerned him. He hoped it wasn't because of Cerplex still. It was like half the noise outside his thoughts was either dulled and unnoticeable or so noticeable that he couldn't focus on anything else. He didn't think about it; he just called. The phone rang once and again before she finally picked up.

"Hi . . . hi . . . are you doing all right?"

"I'm fine. Just woke up from a nap. Are you OK?" What was this? She texted him. Clearly, there was something wrong with her. This conversation was a circle. "Amethyst, you texted me."

"Yes, I did. I just had a question."

"Yeah, go ahead."

"Did your dad know I was running? Like, was he watching me?"

The truth was Sasha wasn't sure. He very well could have been, but he had only mentioned her as a goal recently. As far as Sasha knew, his dad's main focus had been Muse. And Zora was a bonus. "I don't think so. But I need you to listen to me. My dad is trying to find you."

"Since when?"

"He asked me if I knew where you were, and I didn't tell him anything, but he has his ways. I don't want you to go anywhere on your own. Let me help you. Just tell me around where you are."

"How do I know that you're—"

"I'm not being tracked, OK?"

"How are you so sure?"

"I have a TerraTech-enabled personnel phone. I turned off the ability to be tracked."

"I was taken. I'm near Diamond Sea."

"Are you . . . are you with your parents?"

"Just parent."

"Do you feel OK there?"

"I was fine, Sasha, until you told me this."

"You don't sound fine."

"I've had an eventful morning, OK!"

"Did someone hurt you?"

"It's a betrayal kind of day, I guess."

"I'm not gonna betray you." His voice softened at the end. He couldn't help it. He couldn't even find it in him to be angry about it. He had already done it to so many people who considered him a friend. "I just don't want to see anything happen to you. I've already seen it happen too much."

"I'm sorry. I didn't mean you. I meant other people who I'm not gonna name."

"I'm driving now. I'll be there in another eight hours or so. Just stay around other people."

"Are you in Moss?"

"I just left. I'm in a hotel right now. Been driving since three this morning."

"Am I in danger?"

"Yes."

The call disconnected then, and Sasha took it as his cue to get out of bed and get back to his car.

Mask

Amethyst

The cards were stored in a box with acid-free tissue paper in between each one. In the end, Judy left her with $860. Amethyst didn't want to take it, but Judy wouldn't budge, and neither would Zircon.

When they retired to the living room, Zircon immediately left to pick up some food. Judy plopped herself on the couch and slumped to the right. "I'm sure I cut my fingers a couple of times. Too many cards." Judy laughed. Things were quiet for a while.

Judy stared at the mantel before she muttered something under her breath and left the room for a moment. Amethyst didn't know where she went, but she returned with a brown cardboard box with a lid. At the sight of this, Amethyst's stomach began to hurt. She couldn't do any more of this. It felt like drowning in stuff, in memories, and she didn't connect with any of it, and it only made her feel worse of a person.

Judy sat the box on table and began taking out framed pictures. They weren't thick but thin, heavy pieces of black paper shaped frames. She only removed four from the box, but it was clear she wanted Amethyst to look. In the pictures were two girls, the biggest of the two with storm cloud gray eyes and long hair. The youngest was in her lap as they sat on a field. The other, Amethyst, was sitting up, propped by pillows on a gray couch.

The last picture was Amethyst wrapped in a blue blanket. She only could tell it was her because of the name card on the clear bassinet.

"Would you like to keep these?" Judy asked as she took another stack of cards out of the box. Amethyst nodded yes and began picking up the photos, carefully studying them. This was OK with her. This was her own story, the one she didn't remember, but it was nice seeing them. She had never seen a baby picture before this.

"I don't want your last memories of us together being sorted through condolence cards. That's too dark. This isn't about me. This is about the beginning of your life. Once I'm gone, you'll experience the true strength of your gift. I want you to be focused enough on yourself to really use it."

"Why do you have to die for this?"

"Believe it or not, magic is a finite source. It needs to be transferred. You can't just summon it from nowhere." Judy looked sad as she said these words.

Amethyst didn't think of what this experience meant in full. If Zircon was losing her mom at such a young age, that meant that Judy did as well and so on. And finally, it meant that Zircon had waited an extra- long time to experience what she was truly capable of, and it was Amethyst's fault. Amethyst didn't say this out loud for fear that it would make it even real. She didn't want Judy to confirm what she was thinking. Amethyst was hurting enough with what she already know and feeling guilty for not mentally understanding the gravity of it all.

Judy put the pictures back and handed Amethyst the box and responsibility of looking through the photos herself. Amethyst went to her room to put the photos on her nightstand next to the journals she had yet to open. As a start, to get a momentum building, she undid the ribbon on top of the stack. She paged through the top journal, and a receipt fell out. It was dated a month ago. At the top, it read, "Jones and Klide," and one item called A718 priced at $230 Z. Amethyst, curious, looked up what the store was, and she did it a couple of times, not believing the first result.

The receipt was for her mask, two months before she arrived. It was for the exact same style. It was too much of a coincidence for Judy not to order this knowing that she would soon be coming back. How would she even pose the question? *Oh, I see you knew I would be coming back and ordered a mask. How did you know? Did you plan all this? How long did you know?* All these thoughts swam around in her head and made her dizzy.

She heard the sound of Zircon pulling in, and she tried her best to quiet her thoughts and instead thought about the pictures, trying to see them in her mind's eye. She would have to go back down and eat and not think about any of this and focus on the meal. She couldn't take arguing with Zircon again.

Back downstairs, she ate a pizza with them and then excused herself to take a shower. In bed, she held on to her phone and texted Sasha, "U OK?" and "Are you awake now?" After a few moments, she rested her eyes and woke up to the phone vibrating in her hand.

Zora and Muse

Zora

Zora remembered the Falling. She was standing next to a girl in a gym, carrying a bag of basketballs for practice, when Mena Johnson fell as if a change in the strength of gravity had pulled her straight down to the freshly waxed floor. When people began fainting in the mess hall, she couldn't help the sound that ripped from her chest. She stood, half bent, over the guy who had fallen, wondering if she should even touch him; and before she could even finish that thought, they were all at his side, giving him medical attention. After some prodding, the boy began to move, and he was even able to stand. The other two girls came around too, and one even sat back at the table and drank some water. This wasn't what happened then, but she couldn't help the panic that enveloped her.

She stood for a while, frozen in place, as everyone else seemed to continue on. Maybe they didn't remember. Maybe they didn't experience watching their classmates fall from the sky. When they began ushering people out to go to bed, Zora resisted. They didn't prod at her to get her to move or even yell at her, but instead, they let her sit. They brought over water and a pill. Zora cheeked it and finished the water. Residual amounts of the drug began calming her as it slowly dissolved.

In her room, she pulled it out and crushed it between her fingers, spreading the dust among all the other dust at the door from dirty shoes trampling through. When the automatic light shut off, signaling that it was time to sleep, Zora instead sat on the corner of the bed and tried to catch her breath. The action was becoming more difficult these days, and her heart sometimes felt like it wasn't moving fast enough.

The past two days, Zora tried to walk over to the side of the courtyard where Muse sat and looked at the cattails. Muse had removed the string in her hair and let it curl naturally around her shoulders. She looked more natural. She also looked more depressed. To see her was to feel as though you were interrupting a private moment. She wore a constant frown, and her cheeks were always streaked with tears, though no one could say they had ever seen her cry. Zora caught her eye once during breakfast, and she quickly turned away like Zora was standing there naked.

When the morning came, Zora found herself on the floor, unsure of how she had gotten there. She had missed a meal because, shortly after she woke up, they knocked on her door and told her to go into the mess hall for her injection. Everyone was already eating lunch, and a shot had been prepped just for her. It didn't feel like a week had already passed, but she wouldn't be able to refuse it without hurting herself in the process. Even with sleep, she felt utterly spent, and her legs felt heavy with each step. Sitting on the cold bench, the injection was delivered squarely on her shoulder, and this guy was kind enough to offer her a heat pack.

After he left, Zora turned her attention back on Muse, who sat, as usual, alone on the farthest corner of the mess hall. She always ate, something Zora always noticed. Zora got her tray and began making her way over to Muse, taking deep breaths in an attempt to replenish the oxygen she felt her heart needed. Muse thankfully didn't move and didn't ignore her this time. Zora wasn't sure if she could handle it if, after coming all this way, she moved. She sat her tray down in front of her, nearly spilling the juice, and sat. Muse nodded.

"Is there anything you want?" Muse said.

It sounded defensive, and it caught Zora off guard. She had a lot she wanted to say. She looked at Muse for the first time in the eyes for a while and saw only her own reflection staring back. Muse was flat. She wanted to know if she was OK, but that was a stupid question. She wanted to know what was on her mind, but Muse would think that stupid. There was only one heavy thing on her mind that she really wanted to say. She took a deep breath, feeling dizzy. "I'm sorry I got you roped into this. I tried to keep the blame on me."

"It was my idea, my plan. I'm just sad for myself." Muse seemed to peek through in that split second before she bowed her head, picking at the crumbs on her tray. "I don't want you to feel sorry for me. I'm just waiting, Zora, for this to be over."

Zora spoke softly, "I'm not even sure anymore what they're doing. I don't even know what I'm going to be charged with, and no one has talked to me in days."

"Once we're no longer useful, or we die. That's what I've come to realize," Muse said as she took a sip of her milk.

Zora hadn't really considered there might be a natural end to all this. It wouldn't matter what law she broke if she was already dead. The emotion was there, but she was grateful she couldn't deeply feel it. She could only nod so Muse would know she had registered her words.

Zora spoke softly. "You know, I kinda want to just be taken to whoever birthed me. I don't really care anymore."

"I still do. I just don't want to take drugs anymore. I'm ready for any way out."

"Have they told you who your parents are?"

"Yes, and I have elected to not remember the name."

"How? How do you do that?"

"I think really loudly about something else."

"Are you joking?"

"Partially. It helps. Have you been sleeping OK?" Muse moved her tray to the side.

Zora shook her head as if to dislodge the thought. "No, not really. I don't sleep well."

"Me neither. Want to sit with me outside?"

The yard was damp from rain, but the sun was beginning to dry the damp spots from the concrete. They sat on the edge of the fountain. Zora couldn't stop thinking about what Muse said about death. As she sat, with the sun beaming down and the mist from the fountain falling on her legs, deep inside, she could feel the beginnings of panic. This feeling soon became tiring, and she took a few deep breaths to temper it.

Muse seemed less sad in that moment, but there was no mistaking her potential feelings of nervousness as she bounced her leg up and down. Zora, in that moment, wanted to know what she was thinking about. What did her mind naturally shift to after saying what she had said?

Judy

Amethyst

The journals sat for two days before Amethyst even opened another one. She chose the one with the light green cover mostly because its pages were yellowing from age. The first line of every page was a countdown of weeks and days, ending at forty-one weeks and three days. It was a pregnancy journal.

She read the lines that seemed to pop off the page. Every so often, Judy would press into a page. Amethyst guessed she was feeling a strong emotion in that moment, and as a consequence, those words were darker than the rest. She wrote, "The color I can't stand now is yellow. It makes my stomach hurt when I see it. I can't even eat yellow food. And people judge me for making Zircon the elder sister. I don't say, 'It's my second,' to strangers anymore."

And the last line, she read: "I got in a fight with Tim over the name. I just had such a long day." Amethyst stopped when she found she couldn't focus on the words anymore, and she thought it was unfair to keep reading her memories out of context like she was. It was like she was fast-forwarding and rewinding through Judy's life and not experiencing it.

Echoing in her head for the rest of the day was the thought that Judy felt guilty for having Amethyst. Maybe they weren't married yet. Maybe they didn't have the money for another baby. Whatever the case, Amethyst couldn't find it in her to be upset about it. She already had a mom, who wanted Amethyst more than anything.

When she went down from breakfast, she saw Zircon next to Judy, who was lying on the couch. She had blankets piled on top of her and pillows propping her head up. Zircon was refilling a glass of water beside her and readjusting an already perfect stack of magazines.

Zircon gave the orders in a commanding voice. "Can you bring me the heating pad from inside the closet? It's in a clear bin, should be at the bottom. I haven't used it in a while."

"Which?" The question seemed to annoy her, but how was she supposed to know which closet she was talking about?

"The one upstairs, across from the hall bathroom at the very end." Zircon spoke in a kinder tone.

Zircon situated the heating pad under the blankets and pulled up one of the ottomans beside the mantel. She crossed her legs on top of it. Judy looked comfortable. Her hair looked like she had brushed it this morning, though it lay flat on her pillow. Amethyst walked closer, coming around the couch.

"Do you want to sit with me?"

Amethyst said nothing and pulled up an ottoman.

The hours didn't move slowly for Amethyst. They went entirely too fast. Though it was still light outside, the golden hue was still falling on all three of them in the living room. Judy was now asleep but was sweating. Zircon did nothing about this. Amethyst expected something, maybe wiping her head with a damp, cold cloth, but she wasn't sure if that would actually help her or if that was just in the movies.

Zircon's dark gray eyes were low, veiled by her thick eyelashes. The only indication that Zircon was living and breathing was the rise and fall of her arched back and the very rare finger move of her thumbnail running back and forth under her pointer finger. Zircon went to the bathroom at around seven thirty, and Amethyst was thankful for the reprieve. She allowed her body to relax.

Judy turned over on the couch and took in a deep breath. Zircon didn't come back immediately, but there must have been another entrance to the kitchen because she could hear the click of the stove burners being lit. The living room was filled with two scents that intermingled. The first one was an astringent one, and the other was a sweet yet spicy smell. It made the house smell medicinal. Amethyst hoped it was food because she was beginning to feel light headed and annoyed.

Zircon offered Judy food, and she had a couple of spoonfuls before turning over again. Amethyst sat on the floor, using the coffee table as a dining table, nearly gulping spoonful after spoonful. Amethyst looked up midway, expecting Zircon to say something, but she didn't. She placed her own empty bowl on the coffee table and went back to her position, watching Judy.

"If you're tired or anything, you can rest. Mom is just tired right now."

But Amethyst didn't like the word *tired*. It didn't mean nothing would be around the corner. She didn't want to leave. So she didn't respond and went back on her ottoman perch, full and just a little sleepy; her thoughts became quieter. She wasn't focusing on food or trying to find something to distract herself.

She thought about what Judy must be thinking, being watched so closely. She could only hear a voice like someone was calling for her from underwater. She took an internal deep breath and refocused, almost praying to herself that she would hear what Judy was thinking. She saw a yellow flower but no words. She noted to herself that she would ask Zircon if she could see pictures in people's thoughts as well. Amethyst stopped then and tried to focus on Zircon—nothing, nothing at all.

Judy began pulling the covers off herself and unsteadily sat up.

"No, Mom, lie down." Zircon rushed over to put her hand behind Judy's back to support her.

In a weak, almost pleading voice, Judy asked, "Can we open some windows?"

"Yeah, I will. Just lie down." Zircon moved the blankets from her legs as spoke.

The house was soon freezing, and Judy seemed perfectly content with the cold night air that was sweeping in through the windows. She turned back over and fell asleep, her soft snores creating a steady rhythm Zircon seemed to try to match, perhaps for her own nerves.

Amethyst had never seen anyone die before, but she did witness the beginning stages of her father's death. He stood over the kitchen stink, complaining of indigestion. Soon he was retching, and her mom called an ambulance. Mom had her stay behind, thinking it wasn't serious. Her dad died on the way to the hospital from a heart attack.

This was all different. Judy knew she was dying. Zircon knew Judy was dying, and Amethyst knew the death was because of her. She didn't know this woman, but when she couldn't ignore her gut for a split second, she felt the panicked feeling creep over her, tightening her body, making her sitting posture even more difficult. When Judy turned over again in her sleep, they saw just how much she was sweating. The wetness made a triangular collar on her lilac blouse.

Zircon got up then and covered her with a blanket. "You can go to bed. I'll let you know if anything changes, OK?" Zircon spoke into her hands before she lifted her bowed head.

"I'll make some tea," Amethyst said more to herself than to Zircon.

Amethyst chose the tea based on how nice the sachets looked. She couldn't find the tea kettle, so she used a pot and watched as the water pearled beneath the surface and rise. She didn't know how Zircon liked her tea, so she kept her cup plain so she could fix it how she liked.

Zircon now had half her body over Judy. She was taking deep breaths. She walked closer and sat the cups on the table. As Zircon turned her head, Amethyst realized she was crying. Her back was trembling. Her silent tears turned into a soft sob. Amethyst stood there watching her breathing unsteadily that turned into a wail that shook her. Zircon didn't allow Amethyst to do anything. She didn't allow her to comfort her or even cook her food.

Within the hour, the house was filled with people sitting with Zircon. Amethyst sat on a chair pulled from the patio in the corner and watched everything that happened like a television show. Amethyst didn't realize she was shaking until someone mentioned it. Amethyst said she was fine as she walked up the stairs, parting through groups of people.

The people didn't leave until nearly three in the morning, and Amethyst still sat up, too anxious to do anything, on the foot of her bed and looked at the journals opened to various pages and the photos strewn on top of the dresser in front of her bed against the wall. There was a final wail intermixed with the sound of tires pulling away before the house was too quiet. Amethyst didn't see Zircon the rest of the night. And Amethyst finally, exhausted, let her body rest.

Catch Up

Amethyst

The text was only a geographic location, and Amethyst just hoped it would work. The first time, it faded from view because the cell connection failed. Zircon had left to check on things at the funeral home before guests arrived when Amethyst was half asleep. Downstairs, the coffee table was filled with flowers and cards that started to come mere hours after Judy had passed. Crows seemed to have a system down.

Out of the house, the light shifted fast from the bright artificial light of the house to a dreary landscape. It was a short walk into the woods, and her stomach was in knots. On the walk, there was a small group of chipmunks scurrying around a small hill. The grass was wet, and her shoes weren't really meant for the weather.

In her head, she thought about what Sasha would be like now. She wasn't sure how long he had been taking the drug, but she knew from her cousin that the length of time didn't really matter because she had Cerplex in her system for months after she left the "special" school. She seemed constantly fixated on simple things or dazed; there wasn't a middle ground.

Amethyst saw the SUV before she saw Sasha. The tires were covered with mud and the windshield stuffed with flowers from Bradford pear trees. The phone began to buzz, indicating that Amethyst was coming close, and she turned it off a minute later upon seeing Sasha standing back against a tree. He looked utterly exhausted. He walked over, meeting Amethyst right in the middle, and muttered something she couldn't make out.

"I'm sorry." Sasha spoke more into the air instead of to her.

"You don't have to say that. I just wanted to see you. I wish it was under different circumstances but hey. How are you?" Amethyst closed the space between them.

"Very tired, a little hungry. Think it might rain soon."

"What exactly did your dad say?" Amethyst couldn't help feeling a bit irritated.

"He called me, wanting to know where you were, claiming you were in danger and he could help you. I know that's not true. I know exactly how he thinks he could help, and it's just—I think he's losing his mind. He's been researching ways to stop the illness. He's just caught up in it."

"There's nothing he's able to do."

"It helps. It's been helping me for a few years. He knows something."

"He doesn't know anything, Sasha. It's not something that can be cured." Amethyst sighed.

Sasha looked offended by Amethyst's words. Amethyst could not stop herself from asking more questions.

"How long did he put you on the drug?"

"Two pills and an injection. It wasn't long. I stopped taking it. It wasn't like that. It was a few times over the years of another drug, and the pain would stop. It wasn't every day."

"So this was all since high school? Why didn't you say anything?" Amethyst found it hard to catch her breath.

"Yes. He did what he could to help me. What is your problem?"

Amethyst had to stop herself then. She wasn't sure why she was doing this. There was no reason to bring up the past. There was nothing that could be done about it now. It still didn't stop the feeling she was experiencing. It wasn't anger, but it was uncomfortable. Disbelief? Disgust? It felt like a blend of the two. Sasha's dad was more dangerous than she had realized, and though she didn't really experience it before, she was experiencing it now—fear.

It still bothered her that Sasha had not told her about what his father was doing, especially since there were plenty of times he had unexplained episodes of pain just like she did. She had witnessed it. And it was simply not mentioned again. To be perfectly fair, no one was talking about a gene or connecting the dots to the Lost Children until eight months ago, but the students all wondered. Amethyst guessed she was mad because, the entire time, she could have been experiencing it all with him and not alone, wondering.

"I'm just worried." It was not a lie, but it did not truly communicate the depth of what she was feeling.

Sasha nodded yes and seemed to relax then. Gently, he placed a kiss on her forehead. "There's a lot to talk about, and I'd rather not argue. It's been a long couple of days for me. I still don't feel altogether myself," Sasha said as he placed both of his hands on her shoulders.

"You want to come inside?"

Back in her room, Sasha sat on her bed as Amethyst stood by the dresser. She honestly wasn't ready to see him. She wasn't ready to have that part of her life dredged up. Or rather, she didn't want to think about just how backward everything was there. They had no idea about what she knew, and she couldn't tell this to the world. She had no idea what would happen, but she felt in her bones that the Crows already had something in place for those situations. Balancing on her tongue were the words *you aren't sick*, but those weren't good enough. She would have to explain further. Instead, she decided to just tell him what was immediately happening.

"My mother passed away, and I have to go to her funeral."

"Oh my god, fuck! I'm so sorry. Is that why you're here alone?"

"Not my adoptive mom, my biological mom. I'm fine. She was sick."

"But still, Amie, that's terrible."

She knew in that instant that she had to change the subject now. He would think she was crazy otherwise. The truth was she didn't feel a whole lot after it happened but anxiety. She operated on the information that it was meant to be this way, and Amethyst wondered if he could see it on her face. She hadn't been crying. She didn't feel sad. But she did feel a deep urgency to just get it over with and take him to the pond and hope something happened. It was worth a shot. Amethyst told him to follow her, and maybe it was a mix of his exhaustion and perhaps feeling sorry for her, but he followed without any questions.

Mind Numb

Marcus

Marcus stood at the hood of his car at the gas station, looking over the files that were sent via next-day air to him. It was sent directly from Central Glass Hill Precinct. It stated that Amethyst Millen was released into the custody of Zircon Millen. Her adoptive name gave him enough information to find out where her sister lived, and now he just skimmed over the documents, waiting for his food to be done so he could pick it up.

From the last stop, he picked up a map of Diamond Sea, and he surveyed it for spots he could isolate her. She had to go out alone at some point. He would just have to wait for her. From his pocket, his phone vibrated. It was an auto-generated text message informing his food was ready for pickup. He picked up and drove to a park to eat in peace, closer to the beach. In spite of the near-constant drizzle, the day was nice. It was a perfectly cool temperature, and no part of the ground was especially wet that it would ruin his shoes.

Spreading his food across the dashboard, he thought about what she must be doing right now. She hadn't won like she hoped she would. She was now stuck in the Crow Territory with only her sister. She didn't even get parents out of the bargain. Marcus was beginning to feel a little bad for her, but at least for her, she could live knowing she helped her best friend.

This Zircon girl can't be too bad agreeing to take care of her for free for a full seven years.

Marcus was parked just beyond a lake that was shaped like a kidney bean. It was surrounded by gates topped with barbed wire. The signs to keep off the property were an ultrabright shade of yellow that even he could see and read them from his distance. Further still was the indentations of tire tracks and the backside of a small house made of gray stone. If it were not cloudy, perhaps he'd be able to see what was farther in the distance.

The meal was nothing special, just a burger in some fries, but it did leave him feeling much heavier once he was done. He made notes of his coordinates in his cell phone and in his map and began walking around to get his bearings. Marcus followed the tire tracks to another gas station, and further still, he came on a house that could only be Zircon's. It was made in the same style of the one he saw earlier, but it was much grander. It had two stories, a moon gate, and an enclosed patio made from the same stone and with nearly floor-to-ceiling windows.

The house looked empty. There were no cars parked in the driveway. All the curtains were drawn, and no light permeated through, and any light, no matter how slight, would have been more obvious, especially with the lack of natural light. Marcus began turning to walk away when he heard the sound of a door closing further toward the back. He thought to turn around, but he quickly decided against it. He needed for her to be completely alone and be 100 percent sure of it.

In the walk back to the car, it started to rain, heavier but not heavy enough to drench him. When he got closer to the smaller stone house, he saw a black SUV drive toward the city center. He recognized the plates as Zircon's. That was information he had bought illegally.

When he arrived at his car, he began driving in a *U*, avoiding a direct view of the house, and instead a few hundred yards beyond it to camouflage his car among the trees. He hadn't thought about staying through the night, but he would if he had to. The rain began to pour hard for a few moments before completely letting up. He watched the cottage from afar and looked for any sign of a person or people emerging. There was nothing. There wasn't even a bird.

After an hour and the beginning of the sun setting, the lights set up around the house began to turn on one by one. It must have been automated. He was better off getting some sleep and coming back another day when it seemed like they were coming in and out.

In the drive back, Marcus carefully followed the tracks made countless other times by other cars and slowed when he came back to the lake. In the distance, he could see a small dark-haired girl and a much taller blond man wading waist deep in the water. Marcus slowed and began turning toward the path that cut across and went toward the lake. It was a footpath; it wasn't meant for cars but was easier to traverse from being softened by the rain.

Closer now, there was no mistaking that it was Sasha from the curved way he stood over Amethyst's frame, like a gargoyle. Amethyst shifted her position to behind him, and she pulled him hard into the water, her hands on his back and head, forcing his head underneath. Marcus ran, leaving the car door ajar. When he reached the gate, Sasha's body had resurfaced, and he panted hard.

"What the hell are you doing?" Marcus shouted from a distance. Neither of them turned to acknowledge him.

Amethyst was now patting Sasha on the back, who was still breathing deeply, his chest rising and falling erratically.

"What are you doing, Amethyst?" Marcus said, lower this time.

Amethyst turned in that instant, and this disturbed Marcus. His voice barely rose from a whisper. She looked unfazed by him. She stared right through him.

She took Sasha by the hand, and they began sloshing through the murky water together. The turned to one part of the gate and swung the section aside like a door. Covered in water, they stood mere feet from Marcus. Nothing was said for a few moments, but Marcus could tell that there was something different about Amethyst especially. Sasha looked dazed, but that could very well be Cerplex. For some people, it had that effect rather than one of focus.

"What are you doing here?" Amethyst finally said, her voice disturbingly measured.

"You can't help yourself, can you?" Sasha walked ahead of her and stood right in front of her.

"It will take only a minute. Help me hold her down." Marcus said this as he walked close enough to smell Sasha's breath. Marcus leaned to one side, looking carefully at Amethyst's face, mostly looking for any indication that this might be difficult. Marcus didn't plan for Sasha to be here, but he did have things that could incapacitate him if need be.

Amethyst looked scared then, which brought him a measure of comfort, knowing she was somewhat at a loss for what to do. Sasha rearranged his position, so he stood behind Amethyst, and gently, he began to pull her arm, leading her up the hill and toward the path. Marcus followed them, walking at a steady pace.

Amethyst said as she walked up the hill, "Leave me alone," before turning around, looking Marcus square in the eye. Her fist was now balled, and her forehead creased. "I'm not going to ask you again." Amethyst closed her eyes now and her hands now both balled.

There was a second before the splitting feeling began down Marcus's spine and into his skull. All his perception of light dissipated like clouds before everything went dark. There was a strong falling sensation before the voices that surrounded him turned from shouts to mutters and finally to silence.

Half Blessed

Sasha

Sasha pulled Amethyst away toward the path until she started to walk toward the house on her own. The last of him they saw were the tips of his shoes covered in mud. Zircon still wasn't home, so Amethyst didn't think much of leading Sasha to her bedroom. They, as a pair, trailed in so much rainwater and mud on their way to the bathroom adjoining her bedroom that Amethyst felt immediately guilty for ruining Zircon's perfect house.

Sasha didn't say anything, but he seemed to keep a distance from Amethyst as he cleaned himself up and put on clothes he purchased on his way under Amethyst's recommendation. Amethyst showed after, periodically looking at the clock on the sink counter. The funeral would be over very soon, and by the time she got there, her mom would already be buried. She still changed into the clothes Zircon bought her; the house would still be filled with people later tonight.

Sasha had made himself comfortable on her bed, lying on his back. He stared up at the ceiling and took slow breaths.

"Are you hungry?"

"No."

"Do you need—"

"No. Amethyst, I'm fine. Are you OK? Do you want me to leave?"

Sasha said as he rose from the bed, getting up to stand at eye level with her.

"I don't want you to leave me alone. I know it's all your dad," Amethyst said as she pulled her hair back with a hair tie, getting her hair ready to wear her mask.

"Can you be honest with me?"

"It depends."

"Oh, what?"

"Oh, whether you are ready for that information. Some things can't really be explained. They need to be experienced. You should now know that. I've shown you all that I can show you," Amethyst said, running out of breath midsentence, her breathing strained.

"Did you put your voice in my head?"

"What voice? You mean the one at the lake? No, no, Sasha, that just happens. I wasn't doing anything with your mind. I wouldn't even know where to start." Amethyst didn't want to sound rude, but the day had already been such a long one, and she didn't have all the answers right at that moment.

"What did you hear when you had to do that?"

"Your voice." Amethyst now looked down at the mask in her hand, rubbing the fabric between her fingers.

"You don't think there's anything significant to that?"

"I have no idea."

Sasha walked across the bedroom and put his hand squarely on her shoulders. "A few more questions. What exactly did you do to my dad?"

"I projected my thoughts into his head. All I did was think in the direction of his mind. I heard his thoughts at the end as we were walking away, so I'm sure he's OK."

"Can all Crows hear thoughts?"

"No, it's only the ones in my family."

"Why can I hear what you're thinking then?"

Amethyst couldn't register this information right away. She stood, eyes downcast for a while, before lifting her head that now felt heavy just to shake her head no. All she could think in that moment was the simple word *no*—no to everything she had thought in the last day, just no to the thoughts and information that did not immediately fit.

She found herself wanting Zircon to arrive in that moment. She was the last connection she had to anything here and everything that was foreign. Sasha seemed to be clinging onto every word in her head because he nodded along with them.

Sasha said slowly, "I just feel so confused. What you did out there—I saw it in my head what was running through his mind, but I don't understand how you did it."

Amethyst didn't understand how she had done it. She didn't just think that she wanted to do what she did. She only remembered in that moment she felt so incredibly angry. But that wasn't the answer Sasha was looking for, and it wasn't the answer Amethyst wanted to accept either because it meant that she had no self-control. Maybe it was true, but before she went any further with this line of thinking, she started to think how she would explain any of this to Zircon.

"I should go, OK? You talk to her and tell me what she thinks later. You have a lot going on. There's the funeral and—"

"It was going to happen anyway, Sasha. Stay, and I'll talk to her, and then I'll come get you. I need some proof, OK?"

Amethyst made Sasha some coffee and a sandwich as they waited for Zircon and the rest of the people to arrive back from the funeral. Amethyst had no appetite as they waited. Her stomach was in knots as she sat on the edge of the bed, listening for the sound of gravel being pulled under tires. Sasha tried to change the mood of the room by talking about mundane things like what shopping was like in the city center. Amethyst responded that everyone wore mask. This paused the conversation long enough that the silence was broken only by the sound of cars pulling into the driveway.

The overlapping of voices and conversation quickly floated up to the room, along with the sound of the lights being flicked on. Amethyst wondered how long she should say up into her room before she separated Zircon from the crowd. Amethyst decided an hour. An hour was a good amount of time for one to become comfortable. It didn't take an hour.

After a few moments, Zircon was knocking on her door, probably wondering why she wasn't at the funeral and why she was so ungrateful. Sasha hid in the bathroom while Amethyst opened the door and kept her thoughts quiet. "Come down soon," Zircon said in a hush tone, her mask in her hand in her eyes, red from crying.

"I'll be there soon. Can I talk with you?" Amethyst opened the door wider, inviting her in.

Zircon entered the room and sat down, her long black skirt flowing over the edge of the bed.

"I'm sorry I didn't make it. I was dealing with some things here. Sasha's hiding in the bathroom. We went to the lake, and he heard my voice, and I heard his, and we don't know what any of it means."

"Slow down," Zircon said as she wound her mask around her hand. "What were you doing at the lake?"

"Trying to help Sasha like Mom helped me."

"But you aren't his mother. You can't do that for him, but what do you mean he heard your voice?"

"When he was under." Amethyst walked closer.

"I don't understand. What do you mean? Do you mean you projected your thoughts into his head while he was under the water?"

"No, I didn't. He heard my voice while he was under the water."

"That only happens when someone is successfully transformed, Amethyst."

"That is what I did." Amethyst raised her voice.

"I don't know how that is possible, but let me go downstairs for a minute. I need some time to process this," Zircon said as she put her mask back on and rose from the bed. "I'll be back in a moment."

Zircon returned with a much older woman whom Amethyst had never met. The four of them went to the patio, which was now empty with the exception of folding chairs. They closed the door and drew the blinds on the door.

"She needs to speak with you both, and I want you both to keep this information to yourselves for now."

"I'm Eve. I was a friend of your mom before she moved to Diamond Sea. I helped her study her family lineage."

"Nice to meet you," Amethyst and Sasha said in unison.

"Your lineage is a very long line, more than five hundred years. It's stayed intact for so long that, in your case, even though you aren't Sasha's mom, you were able to change him, but it's only because you guys share some familial connection. I don't know how off the top of my head, but you're most certainly related." She smiled as she spoke.

"There's more," Zircon said, sounding impatient.

"Yes, you've created some complications for yourself because Sasha's biological parents now have to participate in a ceremony so they can die, and unfortunately, you are the only one who can perform it." Eve spoke of this so calmly.

"You'll have to do it within the year." Zircon seemed annoyed.

"Yes, there's not much documentation of what happens if this isn't followed, but in the case where it wasn't, the transferrer was the one who passed away to restore the balance. For now, he's simply half blessed like you were before your submersion and therefore partially possessing his gift."

Sasha thought about his biological parents dying in all sorts of ritualistic ways, and Amethyst allowed his thoughts to occupy her own head. She didn't want to think her own thoughts. She didn't want to think. She thought for a split second that she should not have done what she did, but she immediately pushed that thought out of her mind. Sasha had so much of the drug in his system. It was the only way to restore his body to where it was before the process had started. It was the only way to help Sasha be well. Eve nodded yes and held Amethyst's hands in her own as if she was blessing her, blessing the work she would do with them.

Flashing Lights

Zora

In the middle of the fountain was a hair tie that one of the girls lost when they got into a fight with another girl. Zora didn't know their names, but she saw all three of them fall to the ground, panting shortly after the fight had begun as if it was too much expended energy. Zora had been feeling like life had been taking too much energy to do anything.

Muse fainted a few times, so she had been doing worse. In the middle of the night when she could just lie down and not have to worry about anything but sleeping, Zora found that even that took too much from her. She felt like she would die in her sleep, and that would be it. No one would know about this place or what happened to her. No doubt everything would be kept a deep, dark government secret. These thoughts chilled her to her core.

Later the next day, Muse walked up to Zora and laid her head on her shoulder. In a frayed, linen-like quality, she said she could barely breathe. Zora knew that if she made too much of a scene, she would be given an extra dose, so she made sure to keep herself calm as she lifted Muse from the lunch table and walked over to one of the masked men dressed in black. "She can't breathe," Zora said flatly.

They immediately began to crowd around her and then take her away.

The guy she spoke to seemed unfazed by what had just transpired and told her to finish her lunch. Zora didn't make two steps before she fell from the sky and hard onto the floor.

Like flashing lights, the scenes of the inside of an ambulance, a hospital room, and a constant drone of beeping filled her senses and drowned out any thoughts she had. Everything simply happened to her. She felt like she was an audience member to her own life. Faces passed by and came into view like a carousel. Zora tried to completely close her eyes, but a pain was dragging her back in. It was all over and very familiar. There was no telling how long it would last, so she did all she could do, which was breathe out every pulling and twinging sensation.

This pain was deeper. It felt like it was deep in the core of her being, and there was no break between the waves of pain as they overtook her. Nausea was overtaking her at the same time. She rose from the bed, ready for what was inevitable to happen, but nothing came up. She was completely empty. People in all white came in then and surrounded the bed. Within moments, she was restrained. No one in the room looked concerned, and that wasn't a comfort one would think it should be. The restraints hurt.

There was a moment where things seemed to slow down, one of the people in white doing something Zora couldn't see. There was a deep pressure and then a sharp pain that radiated her arm like fire ants. The pain seemed to instantly dull. Zora found she could take a deep breath that actually provided some relief. The suffocating feeling was lifting from her like a heavy blanket.

There was another feeling; this one she realized what it felt like, a needle going into her arm. It made her want to crawl from her skin. It felt like she was itching from the inside. The itching feeling lasted for a few moments before leaving. All that was left was the feeling of the prick from the needle that felt like a hole in her arm.

"You should feel better soon," someone said.

Zora didn't know why, but something about the statement seemed to weaken something inside her. She was already out of that research campus and in what one would consider a normal place, a hospital, and now that she was better, would they already send her back to Turpeek? She wanted to be home and in her own bed, not restrained to one, not locked in a room, drugged up, and staring at hairline cracks on the tile.

What she knew about her predicament was that the only way out was with her birth mother. Zora halfway relented that it would be OK. She didn't know what was on the other side, but she could only look like an older version of what she saw in the mirror and not this monster. Zora admitted to herself she didn't know much about Crows beside the fact that they seemed to be more serious than Bluebirds. Maybe it was an act. Maybe the song and dance was just that.

Sleep rammed into her brain. One moment she was looking at the metal tray that was left at her bedside, and the next moment, there was total darkness. A soft voice was calling for her. Her name was pronounced like Zoe-ra and not Zor-ra like her friends pronounced it. This person was clearly not a friend.

Her eyes fluttered open, and the people in white were back. This time, there was a clear leader who wore a white coat and on it was a metal pin that read Dr. Miles.

"Do you know what today's date is?"

"No."

"Do you know where you are?"

"The hospital."

"How old are you?"

"Twenty."

"Your name?"

"Zora Jo'nest."

Epilogue

A *week later…*

The sun was shining and blazing hot as Sasha and Amethyst made their way down the steep hill toward the lake, around it, and through the woods to the blue trail. If they followed it straight, they would cross the grave site on their right. The only sound was of their feet lifting and falling into moistened dirt from yesterday's downpour.

From the garden, Amethyst picked a few flowers she thought were nice and tied them together with the ribbon from the journals. They looked naked otherwise. When they came on the site, they followed along the rows of graves until they came on *M* for Millen. Her mother's grave was the last one in the row. The headstone was a white marble etched with gold lettering.

Sasha stood back as she paused at the site. Amethyst had never been to a grave site before. She had missed her dad's funeral because it was too much, and now here, she wished she hadn't. There was no one she could watch to see if she was doing anything right. She placed the flowers in the innermost crease where the stone met the ground and stood back, not wanting to step on anything that was her.

"You want to say anything?" Sasha said, walking closer.

Amethyst took a deep breath and touched the stone, feeling the heat from the sun.

"You're gonna see either me soon or some distant relatives."

"That's not funny."

"I'm just talking to my mom. It's meant to be serious, Sasha. I don't think I can do what Eve is asking me to do. Don't even know if it's possible. I've already talked Zircon's ear off."

"Thank you for trying to show me where I came from. I put all the pictures in an album. Zircon found it though. And sorry for not seeing anything you were doing for me sooner."

Sasha was quiet then. And the whole forest seemed to be quiet in that moment. The wind broke the moment of silence as it sliced through the trees. Amethyst said nothing more as she touched the headstone once more and turned back toward the path. Sasha said nothing and followed her as she walked slowly, pausing only to catch her breath at inclines.

The rest of the day seemed to be colored with the rich, earthy tones of the forest, and that was all that their mind went back to when they returned to the house and as they thought throughout the day. Ahead of them was a road very few people had gone down, but as Amethyst heard their thoughts intermix, she knew she had to go down it.

Sasha had half transformed and was now her responsibility to make sure the process was truly complete. She tried not to think of this around Sasha, but she could not help it. And each time, Sasha seemed stressed with the thought. In that moment, she wished she could communicate all that she was feeling and experiencing when she was brought to Diamond Sea to somehow cushion the blow when Sasha had to quickly say hello and goodbye to his parents. It would be just as difficult, and there was no way to prepare him. Maybe it would be easier, and he would have no connection. This was her only hope.

On the patio, Zircon laid out a fresh meal instead of eating the leftover food from the funeral. She commented that it just brought such a dark, sad feeling over her, and new food felt like a new start. They ate, thoughts floating back and forth through the trio but no words. This continued through the night.

www.ingramcontent.com/pod-product-compliance
Lightning Source LLC
Chambersburg PA
CBHW020250030826
48979CB00030B/2769/J